Fruit of the Month

The Iowa Short Fiction Award

Prize money for the award is provided by

a grant from the Iowa Arts Council

Fruit of the Month

ABBY FRUCHT

UNIVERSITY OF IOWA PRESS

IOWA CITY

University of Iowa Press, Iowa City 52242

Printed in the United States of America
First edition, 1988

Book and jacket design by Richard Hendel
Typesetting by G & S Typesetters, Austin, Texas
Printing and binding by Braun-Brumfield, Ann Arbor, Michigan

The publication of this book is supported by a grant from the National Endowment
for the Arts in Washington, D.C., a federal agency. The author also thanks the
Ohio Arts Council for support during the writing of portions of this book.

Some of these stories have previously appeared, in a slightly altered form, in the
Ontario Review, Agni Review, Epoch, Indiana Review, and *The Ways We Live Now.*

Library of Congress Cataloging-in-Publication Data
Frucht, Abby.
Fruit of the month / Abby Frucht.—1st ed.
p.   cm.—(The Iowa short fiction award)
Contents: Midnight—Peace and passivity—Fruit of the month—
Engagements—Paradise—The anniversary—Winter—How to live
alone—Trees at night—Fate and the poet—Nuns in love—The
habit of friendship.
ISBN 0-87745-175-3
I. Title.   II. Series.
PS3556.R767F78   1988
813'.54—dc19   87-28405
                                                                                  CIP

For Michael

and, of course, for

Mom and Dad

Contents

Midnight

Not even my own mother shops regularly anymore. She confessed this to me last week on the telephone. "I just stop in on my way home from the office and pick up some lamb chops or something," she said. "I don't plan ahead anymore. I never know what I want until it's right in front of me and then I don't think twice about buying it."

"That's exactly what we do," I told her. "We just walk to the store after work and get dinner. How are you supposed to know on Monday what you'll want on Friday?"

"That's right," said my mother.

I used to come home from grade school to find her leafing through cookbooks. She owned almost an entire set of Time-Life cookbooks, one for each region of China, France, Africa, and the United States. Once, when she had worked for a week preparing a genuine Chinese feast complete with six entrées, two soups, and various appetizers, my father surprised her with a set of dishes he'd bought at the Metropolitan Museum of Art gift shop. He had skipped work and driven the fifty miles there and back to get them. The delicate soup bowls, robin's egg blue with enameled dragons, were rimmed with gold paint and came with special matching spoons that looked like boats. We dressed for dinner that night and my mother pinned my hair up with chopsticks.

Then one day when I was seven she picked me up at school and took me straight to the supermarket. The second grade had just experienced its first air raid drill; when the alarm rang, instead of filing out to the school yard as we did for fire drills, we were told to sit down in the hallway, our backs to the wall, our knees drawn up to our chests, our hands folded over our heads. It was wonderful. For two full minutes we sat there with our heads thrust between our knees while the teachers, in their high-heeled shoes, clicked up and down the hallway. I spent the whole time staring at my underpants. That afternoon my mother and I filled a whole cart with canned goods—soups, stews, juices, fruits. We bought five-pound bags of wheat flour, white flour, rye flour, and cornmeal and a slew of pastas, including the Popeye spinach noodles I had been pestering her about for months. These were not the types of foods we ordinarily bought and, sensing something unique in the air, like a holiday, I ran to the candy shelves and picked out a bag of Tootsie Roll pops and a carton of Cracker Jacks, which I placed in the cart right under my mother's eyes. It was then that I noticed she didn't share my excitement. She looked agitated. She was talking in low tones to a woman in curlers who was wheeling not one cart but two, one with each hand.

"Peanut butter," the woman was saying. "If you run out of meat at least you'll have something."

"Dried milk," said my mother.

"Tuna," said the woman.

In all there were nine bags of groceries, which my father carried down to the basement when we got home. There was a pantry in the basement, which had a red tiled floor and a bathroom. I had been allowed to paint a mural on the wall beneath the entrance to the crawl space. I painted the flat blue surface of an ocean and, perched on top of it like a buoy, a house. My mother had promised that if I learned how to swim we would move to a house on the water, something she'd always wanted. I couldn't wait. The idea of swimming to school instead of taking the school bus thrilled me. Right out the front door, splash, into the water!

It took a long time to put those groceries away. When everything was in place, we stood for a while gazing at the full shelves, at the rows of bright labels and gleaming tin. We could hear the squeak of my father's shoes as he walked across the floor above us, then the murmur of the television. It was 1962. I was well into the third grade and a Bluefish at the YMCA swim class before we started eating any of that food, and it wasn't until my final year of college that my mother began losing the habit of shopping and the pantry began to thin out. I was home for a visit when I woke up at three in the morning craving a bowl of Campbell's New England Style Clam Chowder. I crept downstairs in my nightgown in the dark, away from the noise of my father's snores, to the basement. There I found one box of cornflakes, a can of water chestnuts, a packet of herb seasoning, and a three-ounce jar of pimentos. Feeling around on the third shelf, I touched something furry and soft. Still warm. My father, just that afternoon, had set some mousetraps. I screamed and ran upstairs to the kitchen, where I called Charlie on the telephone. He was eight hundred miles away in Illinois, sleeping in bed with his wife. If she had answered I would have hung up.

"I touched a dead mouse," I whispered into the telephone.

"My god," said Charlie. "It's two o'clock in the morning."

"So what?" I said. "It's three o'clock here. I miss you."

"No," Charlie said. "I don't have the exams graded yet."

"I want you," I said.

"No. I don't think I'll have them by tomorrow morning either. Just because I give you kids my home number doesn't mean you can call me at two A.M. You can tell your friends that, please."

"I couldn't sleep," I said. "I just want to be holding you."

Charlie sighed. "I suggest you make an appointment with Psychological Services," he said. "I don't mean to offend you, but if you can't sleep for worrying about your exam score there may be some other problem you don't know about."

We just sat there for a little while without speaking, weighing the distance between us. I swear I could smell, through the telephone receiver, the strawberry-scented lotion that Charlie had told me his wife smeared on her body every night before going to bed. After a time he said, "Well," and I said, "I don't know if the breathing I'm listening to is mine or yours."

"That's how it should be," he said.

Finally we hung up and I climbed the stairs to bed, my hand on the smooth woody grain of the banister. I was no longer hungry.

When Charlie left his second wife she threatened to starve herself to death. Lorelei is already thin as a pole and in her hip boots and buccaneer blouses resembles an egret with its feathers ruffled up in the cold. She can't think of herself as a woman, Charlie tells me. She once made the remark that a woman's chest was really, when you got right down to it, no different from a man's. "I don't see what all the fuss is about," she complained. Someone else pointed out that women have breasts while men do not, and Lorelei retorted that aside from that there was no distinction whatsoever. She still lives in the artsy house they shared on Forest Street. We stayed there once when Lorelei went off to Italy; Charlie had made a copy of their house key before he gave his set to her. We spent half the night sharing a bubble bath in the monstrous claw-footed tub, admiring our image in the mirror which covered the opposite wall. Above the tub Lorelei had painted, directly onto the tiles, a picture of a shelf with a pot of Swedish ivy sitting on it. The curled tendrils, with the light exactly right on the edges of the leaves, climbed right up the wall, across the ceiling, and down the smooth face of the mirror. When I reached for a cake of soap in a nook in the wall my hand hit plaster; it was not real soap but a painting of soap, a bar of Dial with a clock still embossed on top.

The house is filled with minor deceptions like these. For instance downstairs, in a long narrow room resembling a Mediterranean sun porch, with tall French windows opening onto a patio, stucco walls with pale blue trim, and a parquet floor, Lorelei had painted, on either side of the fireplace, a set of bookcases complete with editions of all the books Charlie had taken with him when he moved out of the house. *The Origin of Species. The Hammond World Atlas.* A complete set of Peterson's field guides. Krebs' *North American Plant Key. The Double Helix.* When you step into the room to get a closer look, you notice that the shutters flanking the windows are painted as well, but that the fireplace is real and the bars of moonlight on the floor are also real.

"Is she this crazy?" I said to Charlie as we walked from room to room with Lorelei's plum-colored bath towels wrapped around us. "Or is she just having a good time?"

"She's talented," Charlie said. "She's a goddamn genius."

"Let's have a look in the kitchen," I said. I had a vision of a pantry stocked with rows and rows of catsup bottles painted right onto the wood. The cupboard was pine with black knot-holes and cast-iron hinges. I opened it. It was bare.

The best thing about living in such a small town is that you can walk everywhere you need to go, to the bank, movie theater, laundromat, supermarket. Charlie, who is a biology professor at the college, is terrifically proud of the fact that we've filled the gas tank only once since August. He means to set some kind of record. Four tanks in a year. We are having Thanksgiving this year at our house, which pleases him; everybody's coming to us. Last year we had to drive to New York, which spoiled everything.

Each day around five when I finish up at the library I walk across the square, along the treacherous brick walkways, to Charlie's office. I have broken, in the past year and a half, the heels of three shoes, and I'm waiting for the day when I break an ankle and can refuse, under pressure from friends and relatives, to sue the town. We wouldn't sue because we don't need the money; we have everything we want. Our apartment backs up on the campus, on an acre of green with a pond you can skate on in winter. The rent is cheap, heat included. Last winter we pooled the year's savings and rented a cabin on the island of St. John, and when we got back we bought two pairs of cross-country skis. The world's troubles, we agree in private, seem to be passing us by. Each month we send a check to World Hunger. I have noticed that we write smaller checks if we've recently argued or if, for some reason, we haven't been getting along. When this happens we spend the extra money on ourselves. Once, after a week of finding nothing to say to one another, we went downtown and found ourselves buying a couple of egg rings, those silly bracelets of aluminum which, when placed in the frying pan, assure you of a perfectly round egg—like a child's drawing of the sun.

Now that it's autumn and dark by five-thirty, I can stand undetected outside Charlie's office and watch him through the window. He'll be leaning far back in his swivel chair with his feet in their pointed boots propped up on the desk, reading a paper or explaining the day's lesson to a student. He moves his hands while he speaks, his wedding ring flashing. His third. The first was custom-made by a man in Peter's Hollow in New Jersey; it was pocked with craters and had a molten look. The second was wide and flat with Lorelei's name engraved on the inside. He sold them when the price of gold shot up. Ours are very narrow and as simple as possible; he wears his, he says, to keep his students from falling in love with him. It doesn't seem to work. Day after day they appear at his door, their notebooks pressed into their hearts. Who am I to blame them? He looks like the Second Coming, his curls pulled back in a rubber band, his face like the face on the Shroud of Turin, a landscape of shadows and high places. He wears blue jeans, a T-shirt, a vest from an ancient tuxedo, on its false pocket an "ERA Yes" button I pinned there months ago. The vest is threadbare. The students ask him impossible questions. "According to the Darwinian theory of evolution," one of them said to him yesterday, "what is the origin of life?"

I was a student in the class he called Botany 500. He fell in love with my eyes, which are tragic, gray, and heavy-lidded, and with the fact that on our class walks through Chance Creek I wore a man's tweed hat with a feather. On a warm day at Chance Creek all the men took their shirts off and tied the sleeves around their waists except for Charlie, who stuck his T-shirt in the back pocket of his jeans so it flapped behind him. He has love handles, and his chest hairs curl around each nipple like small cyclones.

Standing quietly in his office doorway, I watch him fussing

with the vine that trails from the top of his file cabinet down to the floor. He is dusting the leaves, lifting them one by one and blowing on them, then wiping them top and bottom with a damp paper towel. After that he mists them, and when he sees me standing there he mists me too.

"Thank god," he says, because I've brought him a chocolate-covered doughnut from the bakery. I ate mine on the way over. That way, he thinks I made the stop just for him.

"What's for dinner?" he asks. "I'm starved."

"Tostadas," I tell him. "We have a coupon at home for tortillas."

"Great," says Charlie. "What time is it?"

I pull out my watch. "We'll need to hurry," I tell him. "It's midnight."

This is one of our jokes. My watch is broken. Whenever he asks me what time it is I tell him it's midnight. The watch was already broken when I bought it. I found it at a flea market in Missouri after a canoe trip. Charlie and I had not yet been together and I thought it might move things along if I failed to show up in class for a day or two. The poor man at the flea market was so eager to make a sale that he actually held up a doll for me to look at, one of those talking dolls with strings that pull out of their necks. I asked to see the watch, which was hanging from a shoe tree. The man said it was broken, stuck on midnight, and he opened it to show me. I asked him if he knew when it had stopped. He screwed up his eyebrows and told me a made-up story, how he had been stationed in Hawaii in the forties; he woke up one morning and looked at his watch, but it had stopped, and at that very moment the first bombs fell on Pearl Harbor. I know it was a made-up story because I heard him say the same thing about a coat with no buttons; he told a lady he jumped up so fast when the bomb exploded that the buttons popped off.

Anyway, I bought the watch, which is small and silver with a rose engraved on the cover, and when I got home that Sunday night there was a message from Charlie. "I missed you in class," it said. I have believed ever since that the watch is special, the cause of our good fortune. Sometimes, walking home at night along the trail midway between the woods and the pond, we hear the trilled eight-note call of a great horned owl, or, from the darkened circle of the pond itself, the songs of small frogs. Early last spring Charlie dug a hole in the ground near the pond and stuck an empty coffee can inside; the next night he reached in and pulled out a spotted salamander that had been on its way to breed. It was black, with yellow moon spots along the length of its back and tail. He held it curled in his palm so I could stroke it, then put it down at the edge of the water.

Tonight, above the sloped roof of our apartment house across the fields, there appears a pin point of light, like a hole poked in the sky.

"That's Venus," Charlie says, pointing. He explains that a planet doesn't blink like a star but pierces the black with a steady brightness. "She has no moons," he says sadly.

"Well, you stay out here and keep her company then, and I'll go up and get the coupon," I tell him. He's still standing there, looking up, when I come out.

At the supermarket, half a mile down Main Street, we select a package of corn tortillas, a jar of jalapeño peppers, a hunk of white cheese, a head of lettuce, a can of stewed tomatoes, and an onion. At the last minute I grab a bag of cranberries from a rack in produce. Little by little, over the weeks, I've been stocking up on the ingredients for our Thanksgiving meal. Last night I bought a bag of marshmallows for the top layer of a sweet potato casserole, the night before a tiny jar of pumpkin pie spice. My parents will be staying in the motel in town, my brother and his wife on the fold-out couch in the living room, their two retrievers on the bare striped mattress in the guest room.

Everybody seems to be shopping in our style—the express

line curves past the soap display and up the frozen foods aisle. A lady behind us remarks that if only they would straighten the line out it would move much faster, and Charlie wraps his arms around my belly to keep us both from laughing. Then he puts a finger to my lips and points ahead of us. His first wife, Mary, is in line near the disposable razors. She wears glasses on a chain around her neck. Charlie theorizes that she takes them off whenever she enters the supermarket so that, if she passes him in the aisle, she won't recognize him. She has no cart, just a small tree of broccoli which she holds in both hands like a bouquet of flowers.

At home, still out of breath from walking so fast, I pour oil in a frying pan and turn on the burner while Charlie unpacks the shopping bag.

"Where are they?" he says.

"What?"

"The tortillas."

"What do you mean, where are they?"

"I mean they're not in the bag."

"How can they not be in the bag? We paid for them. You must have already unpacked them."

We hunt around in the kitchen, peering into cabinets and the freezer. Charlie turns the bag upside down and shakes it. Then he pokes a hole in the bottom and looks at me.

"She forgot to pack them," he says. "Call the supermarket."

"They're closed," I say. "They had to unlock the door to let us out, remember?"

"Call anyway."

"Hello," I say, on the telephone. "I was just down there shopping and the cashier seems to have forgotten to pack my tortillas so I was wondering if you would let me in to get them ... No ... No? ... I'd like to speak with the manager ... You are ... Well, what am I supposed to do? ... I don't have anything else. I just went down there to get my dinner and just because your goddamn cashier forgot my tortillas I have to ... I said just because your goddamn fucking cashier forgot to pack my fucking tortillas I have to fucking starve. Your store sucks. You go home and have your shit-ass dinner while I ... He hung up on me."

Charlie is leaning forward on the couch, his elbows on his knees, twiddling his thumbs. "I'm hungry," he says.

"I should call right back and cancel our order for the turkey."

"I didn't even know you ordered it."

"I didn't," I say. "I thought you ordered it."

"Let's not talk about it now," says Charlie. "Let's get a pizza."

There are three pizza parlors in town, one of which we never go to because the owner exploits his employees, and one of which never puts on enough cheese. Fred's Pizza is a block up Main from the supermarket; it has a mural of the Eiffel Tower on one wall, some photographs of tree squirrels on the other. Centered on each table is a candle in a red-tinted globe. Fred works within sight of the tables, tossing the flat rounds of dough into the air. All the way down Main Street, our stomachs rumbling, we share visions of the spinning wheel of raw dough, the platters of shredded cheese and sliced mushrooms, the flat black rings of sliced olives, ribbons of green peppers, pastrami stacked like silver dollars. We don't speak. There are rows of beveled jars of hot peppers and Parmesan and oregano, in the air the smells of sausage and meatballs and garlic. It is suddenly cold—under the street lights our breath clouds up.

A few steps away we can smell it, not the usual smell but something horrible, lime and decay, a smell dug out of the earth. There's a sign on Fred's door: SEWER BACKED UP—COME BACK TOMORROW.

Hunger is like mirth, the whole body pumped full of helium and let go.

"We're about to starve to death," says Charlie, "and you're laughing."

I follow him back up the sidewalk. For a while we trudge along with our hands in our pockets and then Charlie says we'll have to take the car to the Burger Chef, two miles north. He knows how much I hate hamburgers, and I know how much he hates to use the car, so we're even. We have to search the house for the car keys, which are nowhere. We empty drawers, turn the pockets of our blue jeans inside out, check the pegboard in the kitchen and under the mat on the fire escape. When we lift the couch cushion to look underneath, somehow we end up lying on top of one another on the box spring but it doesn't last—we're too hungry. At last I find the keys in the cookie jar.

"You put them there," says Charlie. "You drove last."

"I did not. I would never put the car keys in the cookie jar. You drove last. When we went to the laundromat and it was raining."

Charlie shrugs. "There's no use arguing with you," he says. "Because I know I'm right. And you know it too. You just won't admit it."

"You are not right and I won't admit it," I say. "You can just go eat your hamburgers without me."

"Okay," says Charlie, and he's out the door before I've even put my coat back on. I have to run downstairs and wait three minutes at the end of the driveway before he turns around and comes back for me. The radio is on. They're playing *Maxwell's Silver Hammer,* which Charlie knows is my favorite song. It seems perfectly clear that if they hadn't been playing *Maxwell's Silver Hammer* he would have kept right on driving, up to the Burger Chef by himself. I don't know whether, once there, he would have bought me a hamburger. Charlie drives with one hand on the steering wheel, the other flat on his thigh, one eye on the road, the other on the gas gauge. He is thinking how every ounce of pressure on the accelerator brings us further from the grace of a full tank. If everyone drove like he does, he is fond of saying, there would be no gasoline shortages and hence no wars.

The boy behind the counter at the Burger Chef has an erection. He's a tall skinny kid and so agitated that when Charlie says, "We'll each have two large cheeseburgers, an order of fries, and a Coke," he brings us two burgers, one fry, and one Coke.

"No," says Charlie gently. "That's two *each*."

The boy returns with two more burgers, two more orders of fries, and two more Cokes. He bills us for everything.

"Let it go," I whisper to Charlie. "The poor kid's really distracted."

"I know," Charlie says, and we eat it all anyway.

Venus has gone down, sunk behind the middle school across the road from our building. We can see, through the sloped glass of the windshield as we park, the flat stretch of black sky over our roof, several stars, the clarity that accompanies cold weather. Upstairs I open the refrigerator and look inside. There is a list on the door, of things I need to buy for Thanksgiving, and I've forgotten to cross off the cranberries. My mother sent the list, as a guideline, she said, but I'm adhering to it absolutely. Next to the word "Turkey," in parentheses, she wrote "Twenty Pounds." I am worried that when I call the store in the morning they'll tell me it's too late for a twenty-pound turkey and that I'll have to make do with a ham. I would not be trusted with a holiday again. Charlie has come in and is sorting through the coupons in the coupon drawer, arranging them in piles. He does this every so often. The pile on the right is made up of coupons which have already expired. He flips through it once, to see what we've missed, and throws it away. The remaining pile he divides once again, into foods and nonfoods. On top of the food pile is a coupon advertising twenty cents off on a jar of Presto spaghetti sauce.

"We'll have that tomorrow," I say.

"Tomorrow's Saturday," says Charlie. "I have to go to dinner at what's her name's house."

"Who?"

"Some student who invited me to dinner."

I close the refrigerator softly and look at him.

"I couldn't say no," he explains. "She's suicidal. It says so in her files. And when she invited me over she said she had this great recipe for chicken and if I didn't come she'd kill herself. She said that. What could I say?"

"You could have said, No—if I come over my wife will kill me."

"I'll say that next time," says Charlie.

This has happened before. Each time, I've felt a small explosion in my chest. It makes me sad. Some fragile-hearted student sets a table for two and cooks dinner for my husband. They all make chicken, because it's cheap and easy and there are so many things you can do with it. They are all slightly myopic, like Mary, or a little weird and artistic, like Lorelei, or they have fine bones and bad tempers, like me. Sometimes I wonder, is there anything left? And how do they know she's suicidal anyway? Has she scars on her wrists? Rope burns under her collars? Do they have to pump her stomach periodically? Or does she simply go around saying things like I have this great recipe and if you don't come up and try it I'll kill myself? And what does she look like?

"What does she look like?" I ask.

"Who?"

"Forget it."

"I'm about ready for bed," says Charlie, and he stands close behind me, his chin resting on top of my head. He lets all of his weight go and just hangs there swinging his arms. I lift them up and put his fingers, one by one, into my mouth. I suck on them greedily like a baby.

"Go then," I say, because I want to watch the news on television. Our government, it seems, has approved funding for construction of the B-1 bomber. Our president has said that we need not concern ourselves, that the bombs won't fall on *us*. I don't know what he's thinking of, but listening to this, and to Charlie in the bedroom already snoring, I feel suddenly prepared for anything that might happen in my life.

Peace and Passivity

For a moment it looks as if Susan might fall. She is making her way down the steps, which are narrow and flimsy and made of metal like a fire escape. Snow has fallen through the night, in huge wet flakes that beat against the roof and windows, so the steps are treacherous. She has slung her bag over her shoulder and grips the railing with both gloved hands as she makes her descent, kicking the snow from each step with a vicious swipe of her foot. With each kick there is the sound of an avalanche, a roar followed suddenly by silence. Another roar, another silence. Susan grits her teeth. Her determination might strike Tom as heroic if it did not make him sad. She refuses to use the front steps, which are inside, well-lit, and carpeted, because the downstairs neighbors, whom Susan and Tom haven't met, have not cleaned up the mess their dog made on the carpet a day ago. It smells. Susan won't clean it up herself, on principle, and Tom certainly is not about to clean it because, well, why should he? He is watching her now, from the kitchen window. The metal stairs run flush with the house at a steep diagonal, and he can see her as she passes. She doesn't know he is there. She thinks he is asleep. He pretended to be asleep and then, when she stepped out on the landing to lace her boots, he climbed out of bed and went to the window. He was touched by the fact that she took care not to wake him, that she dressed in the dark and shut the bathroom door before brushing her teeth. But he really wanted to see if she would kiss him good-bye, even though she thought he was asleep. To kiss a sleeping person, Tom thinks, especially if that person is your husband, is an act of faith and devotion, a form of prayer. So he lay there making grunting dream sounds and waiting. He felt like someone standing on a highway with his thumb out, waiting for a car that would not materialize.

Now she loses her grip on the icy banister and slips. There is a moment of terrible uncertainty: will she fall, or won't she? This is all Tom feels, the tension of the moment, but he feels it in his chest, in the region of the heart. He feels it as love. He

19

reaches out as if to steady her, but his hand smacks the window, and by then she has regained her footing. She is a big girl, five seven, bigger than Tom. He is often reminded of a statue, a figure carved by an artist so in love with the male form that he endows even women with the attributes of men. She has broad shoulders, a wide back, a tight waist, and smooth hips. Her breasts are high and firm, like the pectorals of a body builder. Her thighs, when he lies between them, grip and rock him, and her flesh itself is of such substance that he cannot feel her ribs, or her heartbeat, through it. Lately he finds himself concentrating on her most delicate features, her lips and eyebrows, those two blonde tapered arches, with a nostalgia as acute as that felt by someone staring at a photograph of an absent lover.

Now she is sitting in Jeremy's car in the parking lot, drinking coffee out of a thermos. It must be coffee, because it is steaming. The car's interior is brightly lit. Everything else is in darkness. It is five o'clock in the morning. How long has Jeremy been sitting there, in a lit car with the engine off, freezing his butt? Tom doesn't like Jeremy. He calls him Germie. He doesn't like a man who wears a tank top in the middle of February and rolls his *r*s when he says "Roberto." Roberto is Germie's lover, a tough cookie. It is clear that Germie is complaining about Roberto right now, because Susan is shaking her head and patting him maternally on the shoulder. If only Tom could hear her. How does she phrase her sympathy? He doesn't know. He could be on Mars, looking down at her.

The night before, just as the snow was beginning to fall, they had driven to the mall to get Tom some underwear. He has been putting on a little weight, and he read in Ann Landers that tight underwear can cause sterility in men. Susan made a joke, about cheap, effective birth control, that stung him. She agreed to go along on the condition that while he was in Sears shopping she would stay in the arcade and circulate her petition, against a buildup of the U.S. military presence in El Salvador.

In Sears, he bought the underwear and a bag of milk chocolate stars. He ate them before going out to meet her. She was sitting on a bench, gesturing and talking to a child in a stroller. For a minute Tom thought she was trying to get the child to sign her petition, but then he saw how miserable she looked and that she had crumpled the petition into a ball. "If there's a war," she was saying to the child, "and your daddy goes away and never comes back, it won't be my fault." The child giggled. Susan shrugged and got up.

"First of all," she said in the car, "I'll bet you nine out of ten of those idiots in there never even heard of El Salvador much less Alexander Haig, and then the manager comes up to me and says if I don't stop soliciting he can have me arrested. Soliciting! Then I asked him if he would sign anyway, as long as I had him interested, and he crumpled it up. I could have *him* arrested." She was driving a little crazily, skidding on turns and braking so suddenly he had to brace himself. "I got six pairs of Fruit of the Loom," he said, in an effort to calm her. He unwrapped the package and held them up, but she wasn't paying any attention. She was swearing at a driver who had passed and cut her off at an intersection. "Goddamn ignorant asshole," she said.

Tom stared at the labels on his underwear, at the tiny bright clusters of fruit. It hadn't always been like this; when they were married, a year and a half ago, she was still in school, in classics. At night she read Latin aloud in her study, a corner of the living room she had roped off with a tapestry. Often he would creep up behind it and listen, barely breathing, his cheek brushing against the coarse grain of the cloth. Her voice was husky and melodious, and the strange fluid sounds of the dead language filled him with awe. He confessed to her once that he did this, that he listened, that her facility stunned and moved him. She seemed put off. She began to read in a whisper. Later, as she became more and more political, as the El Salvador thing became, as she put it, an imperative, he blamed himself.

Home from the mall, she announced it was bedtime. She said Jeremy would pick her up at five in the morning and they would drive to Chicago for the workshop and rally. Tom hadn't known anything about a workshop. It was one and a half days long, she explained. It was organizational. Tom said he thought she was already pretty well organized; wherever he went he saw posters with her name and number printed on the bottom. People called, and she directed them to meetings, arranged car pools, and raised money for speakers. She was hardly ever home. When she wasn't home and the telephone rang, Tom didn't answer it. He was tired of the words "El Salvador." El Salvador was two thousand miles away. When Susan said this, *two thousand miles,* she made it sound like next door, like she could look out the window and see it. She was increasingly preoccupied. She had lost her sense of humor. He joked with her now. "Don't do anything with Germie that I wouldn't do myself," he said. Susan yanked off her socks and climbed into bed and curled up facing away from him. She was flexing her feet, arching them, then pulling them taut. The pressure of her toes against his thigh aroused him, and he turned to her and began making love to her, coaxing her. He felt some resistance, but he had learned to recognize in it an aversion not to himself but to pleasure, as if her pleasure were a slap in the face of the world's pain, so he kept on. Her face was wet. When she came finally it was with a vengeance, with a hoarse grieved sound like a battle cry. Her eyes were open, staring past him. He bent closer and whispered. "Peace," he said.

Now she and Jeremy have driven away. The apartment is cold; the heat was turned low for the night. Under his bare feet the linoleum is gritty. He can go back to bed and sleep until work, or he can put on a robe and slippers and drink coffee in the kitchen with the television on. What kinds of shows are on so early in the day? He switches on the set, and stands in the chilly darkness waiting for the picture. At last it appears, a gray aureole rimmed with black, a bull's eye. He turns the volume up until the room hums with static, with an otherworldly sound like an intergalactic message. For the first time his nakedness begins to get on his nerves, and he goes into the bedroom and puts some blue jeans on, and some boots, and his leather bracelet, and then he flops down on the bed and falls asleep. He is wakened by *Good Morning America* in his kitchen. He has left the set on full volume. The noise is enough to blast the cockroaches out of the walls. Sure enough, a door slams below and the new neighbor comes charging up the steps and starts banging on the door. Tom doesn't get up right away. He will wait until the yelling begins, so he will know what to expect, a man or a woman. It's a woman. He goes into the kitchen to pour himself a glass of orange juice, and then he carries the orange juice into the living room and opens the door. Before him stands the neighbor he has never seen. She has dark hair parted on the side and pinned carelessly in back like a flower. She would be pretty if she were smiling.

"It's seven o'clock in the morning," she says. "Could you turn that down please?" Tom admires her control. He can see that she is on the verge of some kind of collapse. She could be the lady in the Anacin-3 commercial, except that under her robe she is naked. He knows she is naked because otherwise she would never have buttoned her robe so meticulously; it has tiny pearl buttons from bottom to top, like those of a bridal gown. "Please," she begs. Someone on *Good Morning America* is yelling about bed-wetting. Tom has to think fast. He puts his finger to his ear, smiles, shakes his head, puts the finger on his neck, shakes his head some more, and opens his mouth wide. The neighbor squints. Her confusion is charming. She peers into his open mouth as if searching for a clue. Tom can see the crow's feet at the corners of her eyes. She is twenty-eight perhaps, older than Susan and smaller, naturally. Her face suddenly brightens. "Oh," she says. "That's *loud. Loud.*" She accompanies the word "loud" with a grandiose gesture toward the kitchen, and then she claps both hands over her ears and says it again. *"Loud."*

Tom fakes a look of surprise and recognition. He hands her the glass of orange juice and dashes for the television, switching it off. The silence is heavenly. In the living room his neighbor is nodding and gulping the orange juice. She hands him the glass, emptied. She points at her chest and yells, *"Carmen."* What a beautiful name. Tom has never heard such a sad and lovely name. It suits her. She repeats it. "Carmen." He grins and bows. When she is gone, when she has navigated the steps past the smelly black lump that is her dog's fault, he slams the door mightily.

This is what Tom does at work. He sits at a small table inside a small office in the topmost floor of a decaying building at the university. The building is called January. The office was originally intended to be a darkroom, and in fact was a darkroom for several years a long time ago. Black paint covers the windows. When Tom is inside with the door closed, a tiny red light blinks on in the hallway, assuring the world of his presence. He has to work at the table because the counter space is occupied by two large flat sinks and a collection of vials, glass platters, and obscure photographic equipment. On a shelf above the counter are some chemicals in squat brown bottles. Some of the bottles are marked "Poison," with a tiny skull and crossbones on the label. There is a box of measuring spoons, a ladle, and a half empty jar of Pond's Cold Cream. For this reason Tom suspects that the photographer was a woman. The presence of the ladle mystified him until he found, in a cabinet under the sinks, a hot plate and an envelope of instant soup. A white lab coat hangs from a hook on the door on the inside. In the pocket of the coat is a small black plastic comb of the sort you see on drugstore counters. Tom has studied the comb for further clues to the identity of the photographer, a hair perhaps, red or blonde. He found nothing. He has been instructed not to disrupt the placement of the objects in the room, as if its occupant might someday return.

Tom's employer is a sociologist whose research is funded by a grant from the National Science Foundation. The nature of the work escapes him. Each week the sociologist brings him a list of numbers to be punched into a calculator. It is important that he enter each set of numbers twice, or until the sums match exactly, to avoid the possibility of error. Once this has been accomplished Tom performs a variety of statistical tests, following the instructions from a book the sociologist has given him. He prints the results in a spiral notebook with a romantic scene depicted on its cover—a couple silhouetted by a sunset on a beach. Perhaps the sociologist was at one time in love with the photographer. Perhaps he is still in love with her. On Friday evenings he opens the notebook and checks Tom's figures, and then he rips the page out and takes it away with him.

The funny thing about this job, Tom has decided, is that it requires no thinking at all but such absolute concentration that if he does start thinking about something, about anything, he will get himself in trouble. He will punch in the same number twice, or repeat a step in an equation, or press a key next to the one he intended to press. Ordinarily things go as well as can be expected. Tom allows himself only the most fleeting of sensations; a pang of hunger, an appreciation of the smooth concave surfaces of the calculator buttons under his fingertips. At the end of each day, stepping from January Hall into the fresh transparency of night, he feels buoyant and lucid as a person who has been coaxed into a trance and made to forget his troubles.

But already this morning is different: Susan has left, she has gone to Chicago, he will never see her again. He has devised a scenario. In the middle of the night she and Jeremy will hitchhike to El Salvador, where, in exchange for a roll of blankets in a cave above a rural outpost, they will smuggle weapons to the guerrillas. They will not make love, of course. They will love only the people of El Salvador and they will carry this love between them like a sacrificial animal. They will share, with the guerrillas, ribbons of beef cooked over a circle of flames. They will forget to speak English. At night they will bathe in the muddy waters of a river whose banks are lit with gunfire.

All day the vision haunts him, but he pushes it back and keeps working. He is performing a Spearman Rank test, arranging the numbers in columns to be paired and correlated. Susan has bartered her wedding ring for a cake of hard brown soap which she rubs between Jeremy's shoulders. In turn he clears a path for her in the jungle, swiping at the undergrowth with his machete. Is there a jungle in El Salvador? In his frustration Tom clears the calculator before completing the test, erasing the afternoon's work. It is five o'clock. The sociologist is furious. He needs the data for the weekend—he is writing a paper. Tom has to start over. At eight o'clock he still has an hour to go. His head hurts. At nine when the work is complete he realizes that he hasn't eaten anything. He opens the cabinet and pulls out the hotplate, plugging it in. He fills a pot with water and empties into it the contents of the envelope. It is vegetarian vegetable soup. The tiny cubed vegetables plump up when the water begins to steam. He drinks from the ladle in measured sips. On the rim of the ladle is something he hadn't noticed, a narrow pink smudge of lipstick. As he eats, dipping the ladle in and out of the hot, fragrant broth, the smudge disappears.

He takes the elevator down. Susan and Jeremy are drinking wine from a pouch made of leather. The wine is cheap and grapey but it tastes of leather. It leaves a purple stain on their lips and tongues. Tom cuts across the quadrangle along shoveled walks to a lot where his car is parked under a lamp. But why go home? In the entrance to a building across the lot is a throng of students lining up for a movie. He joins them, pulling a dollar from his wallet. During the film, he eats Milk Duds from a box in the lap of a woman sitting next to him. The woman gets up and moves to another seat in another aisle, on the opposite side of the theater.

Saturdays are lazy days. Tom sets out to do nothing as if nothing were a task for which he would be held accountable. He sleeps late, waking and sleeping and waking again, and then he shaves, brushes his teeth, opens the curtains, sniffs the air, dresses, lights a cigarette, and sits on the bed to wait. He waits for inspiration. Perhaps it would be pleasant to spend the day in the sauna at the university. There are always groups of young women wearing swimsuits in the sauna, engaging in the kind of intimate but stagy dialogues they have when they know they can be overheard. "I know she knows," one of them will say. "She does?" says the other. "Yes. By the way she looks at me. But I haven't told *him* about it."

Tom will sit in the steamy enclosure until he can no longer breathe and has to go out into the locker room for a cold shower. Then he'll go back in and watch the girls, who are massaging their legs and arms with natural sponges. Or if he doesn't feel like sitting in the sauna he might drive the car into the country, into farmland, following a series of right angles on the straight, narrow paved roads until he ends up back where he started. And once last month, when Susan had cramps and had to spend her entire Saturday reading in bed with her legs propped up on a stack of pillows, he spent the day in bed with her, joking, pretending he also had cramps. She was taking Darvon, so he took one too. He enjoyed the heady feeling it gave him, that feeling of distance, of removal from his body, a feeling that, by swallowing the gaudy orange capsule, he had cured himself of a pain of which he had been unaware.

Or he can go to the Treehouse Restaurant. The Treehouse Restaurant has four unmatched tables and a counter with a row of bar stools covered in tatty blue vinyl. Tom always orders two hamburgers and a Green Garden Salad. The hamburgers are square. He doesn't go there for the food. There's a waitress, a

Plain Jane named Leslie. She has open pores, and she wears thick-soled white nursing shoes and a crucifix, and she thinks Tom is in love with her. He makes a point of inviting her to sit with him while he eats, because of course she will have to refuse. She wears pancake makeup; in the fluorescent light of the diner her face is a pale shade of orange. The last time he ate there he left her a $3 tip on a $3.50 meal, and she came clomping down the sidewalk after him, waving the bills and shouting. She got all out of breath, her whole body quivering under her apron. She would be easy to love, if you were that kind of man, if you were lonely and needed taking care of. "Wait!" she said. "You must have made a mistake." Tom said *yes,* he *had* made a mistake, and he pulled out a fourth bill and pressed it into her hand. She blushed and lowered her eyes, and then she raised them again to look into his face, but he turned quickly away and walked off. Leslie has become, over the last couple of months, a rainy day entertainment, like a Saturday matinee.

Now Tom is crouched before the dresser, rifling through the drawers. He has taken all of his shirts out and thrown them on the floor. Then he lifts them one by one, shakes them frantically, and stuffs them back into the dresser. He is looking for his Saturday shirt, a worn blue denim workshirt on which Susan embroidered, before they were married, a purple half moon and a circle of yellow stars. He wears this shirt whenever he goes to the Treehouse Restaurant, for Leslie's sake; however simple she may be, she will recognize in the embroidery the handiwork of a woman. But the shirt is nowhere in sight. It is not in the closet or in the dining room or in the laundry or under the bed. Tom stands still in the center of the room and shuts his eyes. He likes to think that by concentrating emphatically on whatever he is looking for he will find it—or, rather, it will simply appear. In a rerun of *The Twilight Zone* everyone kept wandering into the fifth dimension, a never never land of fog and creepy music, and he imagines the shirt in that vast empty place, waving its sleeves. Susan is in there too. She is cutting her hair. She is hacking away at her hair with the curved white blade of a clam shell. Are there clams in El Salvador? It comes to him suddenly that Susan has taken the shirt with her; he remembers now, how she rolled it up and put it in her bag. It fits her just right; it is too big on him. He is pleased and then saddened by its absence; on chilly nights she will wear it and be reminded of him.

The Treehouse Restaurant is three blocks north along a road they are widening, and he walks where the sidewalk once was, ankle-deep in black snow in a rut. He would hitch, but no one ever stops on this road because it's so narrow, and anyway he is thinking about ducking into the shopping center and buying a valentine for Leslie. Valentine's Day was two weeks ago so the cards are half price. He buys a small heart-shaped box containing four pieces of chocolate nestled in foil, for a dollar. But the lady at the cash register has a black eye and looks so brave and so deeply hurt that he cannot stop himself from offering her a piece of the chocolate. She hesitates. She has graying hair, no lipstick, she could be anybody's mother. "Take it," says Tom. "I mean it. I want you to have it." He has to eat one himself to show her it's all right. When she bites into the chocolate, a tear wells up in her good eye, and she turns away to dry it with a tissue. Tom hurries off, leaving the box on the counter.

Leslie must have seen him coming from a distance—his table is set, there's a cup of coffee with a saucer on top, his hamburgers are sizzling on the grill. He tastes the coffee. She has sweetened it the way he likes, with three envelopes of sugar. No cream. She is not around. She is in the basement probably, in the bathroom under a light bulb, freshening up. Once, when he came in unannounced, her slip was showing. Finally she appears. She is carrying one gallon jar each of mustard and catsup, and she doesn't look at him, of course. Her rouge is crooked, one cheek higher than the other, and the tips of her fingers, when she comes to take his order, are stained pink. It's cute that she takes his order even though she always knows exactly what he wants. Also, that she always brings him French dressing even though he orders Italian. She has them confused. Today, when he orders French, she brings Italian, which is what he has in mind. He says, "Thanks, beautiful," when she sets the food in front of him. She blushes. He asks her how Dolly is. She says Dolly is fine. He doesn't know if Dolly is her cat or her mother. One of them is named Dolly, the other is Dotty. Either Dotty or Dolly has a cataract, and the other one walks in her sleep. "How's Edith?" he says. Edith, he knows, is a canary.

"She's okay," says Leslie. "You should ask me how I am. I have a toothache. I have to go to the clinic. I have to get off early today." She blushes when she says this, about getting off early. She picks a rotten piece of lettuce out of his salad and drops it in the ashtray. Then she picks the ashtray up and empties it into her apron pocket. He has never seen anyone do this before. He feels sorry for her. The thing is, when he started in on her a year ago he thought she would know he was teasing, but that's the sad part—she never caught on. And now it's too late, if he played it straight he would hurt her. So this is how it is. She dyed her hair. It used to be brown, now it is blonde. Also, when she writes thanks and her name on the back of the check, in her neat looping script, she includes her last name so if he wanted he could look her up in the telephone book.

"I'll walk you to the clinic," he says.

He had never quite realized how solid Leslie is. They are walking in the snow, across an unused lot on the way to the clinic, and he has taken her arm and now she is leaning against him. She is heavy and the snow is slippery. He worries about falling. She is talking about Dotty, about how Dotty bumped her head on the refrigerator one night when she was sleep-walking. But at the door to the clinic she is silent. She doesn't let go of his arm. He knows he is expected to kiss her. But where? On the cheek? He can see, in the smoked glass pane of the clinic door, their reflection. They look like square dancers waiting for a chance to skip down the aisle together. "Well, I better be going," she says, without moving. He bends to kiss her forehead. It is smooth and cool, a surprise. When she goes, when the door clicks shut behind her, it is later than he thought and he is lonely.

Now Tom is standing in the lot outside his building, flexing his arms. It is six o'clock, the world is black and white, all darkness and snow. He has a plan. After dinner he will drive to the university and climb the steps through the gym to the weight room, where he will watch the students lifting weights. He will sit on a mat with his knees drawn up and his hands on top of them, inhaling the twin smells of metal and sweat. He likes the sight of the girls in their leotards and sweat pants, lifting the smallest barbells up over their heads then down and then up again. He has already purchased his dinner, a chicken pot pie and a bottle of Coke. At the check-out line in the supermarket, paying his dollar and change, he thought, I am in training for the single life. He wanted some lettuce but the girl in produce said no, she could not cut a head of lettuce in half for him, he would have to buy the whole head.

Something funny has happened. The dog mess is gone. There is a bleached-out spot on the carpet, like a flaw in a photograph. He crouches, touches his finger to the damp spot, and sniffs. There is a smell of vinegar and detergent, Susan's recipe for stains. Looking up he can see, through a crack at the base of his door, a dim gauzy light.

She is not in the front room, but her coat and boots and scarf and gloves are spread out on the floor where she dropped them in passing. There is a folder, petitions spilling out onto the seat of a chair, and in a pile in the hallway her blue jeans and a T-shirt. The sight of her clothing makes him nervous, as if he's entered a house in which everything, somehow, has been left undone, half finished. He remembers a book he read over and over as a child, about the volcanic eruption in Pompeii. Archeologists, digging at the site, found a half-eaten meal on a plate on a table, a boiled egg and loaf of bread turned to stone. His unease heightens when he reaches the bedroom. There, on the unmade bed, on a landscape of crumpled white sheets, is her bra, the matching hills of black nylon gleaming in the filtered light from the living room. In the hallway—her underpants, a wad of tissues, a sock. He finds her asleep in the bathtub, her head resting on the shoulder of porcelain, her neck arched, her mouth slightly open, her knees raised and spread, the smooth curve of her belly rising with each breath above the surface of the water and then sinking below it. He can see a vein in her breast, a suggestion of blue beneath the globed flesh. She has lovely skin. He has told her this: you have skin like the skin of a woman in a fairy tale. But how defenseless she looks, one hand in the water, one hand out, her blonde face eclipsed by his shadow.

She is dreaming. He can see her eyes hard at work under the lids, darting here, darting there. Nothing else changes or stirs. She is far, far away in a dream. He bends closer to look, and closer still, and he stares at her eyes as if by staring he might follow her and go where she is going.

Fruit of the Month

I went strawberry picking with June in her pickup truck ten years ago, in May. Late May, in Virginia. June came early, before Jack got home from work, so we left without him. I left a note on the door. When I get back, said the note, I'll make us some strawberry daiquiris and we'll sit together on the porch and drink them all night long, listening to mosquitoes. The nature of my notes to him was always, and still is, piquant, because he likes them that way. He is a sentimental man; he keeps my letters in a shoebox tied with string. In the dark interior of the box the ink doesn't fade, nor does the paper deteriorate. Every couple of years he replaces the string, which turns gray from being so often tied and untied.

June said she knew a place where we could get the strawberries free. I said, "Illegally, you mean?" and she said, "Well, yes." If we took the freeway east a couple of miles and then turned off on a dirt road we would come to the edge of a commercial farm surrounded by barbed wire rolled up the way they do it during a war, but further on, just where the dirt road ended near a creek, there was a tree you could climb. By climbing this tree and shimmying out along one of its branches you could scale the barbed wire, dropping down just on the other side of it into the strawberry fields. June wore her hair very long at the time, blonde and fine with a touch of a ripple, like the stuff you peel off corn ears. Even now, if I am shucking corn, I think of this. How I looked up from the strawberry patch, from my knees where I had landed, and saw June scaling the barbed wire after me, her long bare legs straddling the tree branch, her hair covering her face. It was a hot afternoon, and the scent of greenery was sharp in the air, and I have never forgotten it. We squatted together between the steaming furrows of earth, pinching the berries and eating some. "If they don't come off at once in your hand," June said, "leave them on the stems to ripen for next time."

We dropped the berries into a book satchel she was wearing on a strap over her shoulder, and after a while the khaki canvas, bulging with fruit, was stained pink. Our fingers were pink, and our knees, and the edges of our mouths. In the distance, across the shimmering acres of strawberry leaves, like water in the sun, we could make out the wide-brimmed hats of the legitimate berry pickers, and beyond them the low white building where the bushels were weighed and paid for, where the cars were parked. Children played and shouted along the perimeter of the farm, and people gathered on the hoods of their cars to talk and sunbathe. We stayed low and quiet, hoping we wouldn't be seen.

I tired quickly. My legs and lower back ached, and my neck and arms stiffened. I blamed my fatigue on the heat and on my period, which had started that morning. I felt heavy and bloated and entirely out of whack. My head hurt. Finally I lay back on my elbows and told June to go right on picking without me; I was perfectly happy simply to be there. I think I fell asleep. Time passed. The sun got low. The crowd thinned out. When I opened my eyes the first thing I saw was a ladybug that had landed on my stomach. It was opening and closing its small spotted wings in a rhythmic way. One two. One two. I thought of the nursery rhyme, and then immediately of Jack, who would be waiting for me, probably standing near an open window with a tall glass of ice water, sipping and watching the road. His lips would be cool, and his eyes troubled. He keeps his anger inside, in what I've begun to call hot storage, and allows it to surface only in the face of a more worldly injustice. By then it has boiled and sweetened and grown thick. A few days after I went strawberry picking he threw our hairbrush at Ronald Reagan, who was president at the time. Reagan was on the news. He was saying he supported the *E* and the *R* but not the *A* of the Equal Rights Amendment, and Jack got mad and threw our brush at the television screen, breaking it. The brush, I mean. I reattached the handle with duct tape, and we still use it.

When the ladybug had flown off, I sat up and saw June straddling the branch again and munching on a strawberry. She grinned down at me. I was still exhausted and my only inclination was to lie back down and sleep some more, but I pulled myself up, and let June pull me up into the tree. She had scratched her leg on the barbed wire; there was a thin trickle of blood. We made our way across the tree and back down to the pickup. June turned the radio on. The song was *See You in September.* June leaned over and took my head in her hands and kissed me, first on the eyes, then full on the mouth. I was surprised. I responded. Then she said, "There, I've been wanting to do that," and she drove me home.

I told Jack about this later, over our daiquiris. He was on his third, but I was still toying with my first, because I still felt weak and knew if I drank much more I would get sick. Also, I knew I would be driving out to Norfolk early the next morning to go sailing with June on her brother's boat. Her brother was wealthy and out of town. I told Jack that June's brother's boat was small, big enough only for two. I considered this to be a white lie. I also told him about the kiss, saying how shocked I had been. Jack was entirely silent. He stirred his drink, and watched the moths that were beating against the light bulb, and lifted, by arching his foot, a tennis ball that had rolled out from under his chair. That tennis ball has always been a mystery; neither one of us plays and we've never figured out how it got there. He straightened his leg with the ball wedged in the arch of his foot, then spread his toes apart and let it fall—over and over until it bounced out of reach. Then he put his drink down on the cement, but gently, so there wasn't a sound, and went inside. I followed, the screen door banging behind me. He filled a teacup with strawberries, sprinkled it with sugar, and carried it upstairs. He put the teacup on the night table. I began to undress him and we showered. Jack said, "Your fingers are pink." That was all he said. We toweled ourselves dry and lay down in bed, our arms slung across each other's necks. I watched him sleep, as June had watched me. Jack has remained entirely silent in fact, about all of this, for years.

The drive out to Norfolk was long and agitating, twenty-five miles on the highway stuck behind some drunken slob in a Winnebago. He had opened the back door and stood with one foot on the fender, in a stained T-shirt and shorts, guzzling beer, then tossing the empty cans out onto the highway. All this at fifty-five miles per hour. The beer cans soared crazily in the hot morning light, then veered and bounced off on the shoulder abreast of my car. I was afraid to pass him—what if he fell off?—and I never did get close enough to read the license plate. I slowed to forty, until the Winnebago was a speck in the distance, then sped up till I was close enough to have to slow down again. I hated that man. Eventually I lost him, thank god, and got on my way, but the Hampton Bridge was jammed with traffic, everybody headed for the beach. So it was nearly ten o'clock when I pulled into Norfolk, along a road that skirted the harbor, past the convention center and into the slums where June lived. I had never been there before, and I'll tell you right now that I never went back. The narrow street was pocked with craters. June's building was broad and tall, wood frame with row upon row of small windows, some of them broken, the ancient panes warped. I parked across the street, in a lot strewn with rubbish and whiskey bottles, behind a church that looked fire bombed. June's truck was there. I hurried across in my clogs and running shorts. I felt like a child in a war zone. The door was locked. A second door was also locked, so I sat down on the hot, gritty stoop and waited to be let in. In the ten minutes that passed I thought about getting back into my car and driving home, but the harbor, several blocks up on the other side of the road, was just visible, dotted with sails. Besides, I was hungry. June had promised me breakfast. Strawberry pancakes and coffee, she'd said. Finally a man with a cat in his arms came shuffling up the steps and pulled out a key.

Inside was a wide hallway and three sets of steps, each more dilapidated than the last. I chose the steps with the working light bulb. June lived on the third floor, down a hall lined with green doors and covered with old gray linoleum. The linoleum had buckled, and as I walked along, it made obscene noises under my feet. I wondered how June could live in such a place. I hadn't known her very long, having met her through a friend, and that she lived in such a seedy spot excited me. Then, when I knocked and there was no response, I thought perhaps she had mistakenly given me the wrong address, the address of a friend or relative she had been thinking of. I jiggled the door knob. It turned, and the door opened but was blocked after several inches by a chain bolt. I peered inside. The room was in disarray. Books everywhere, and clothes, and a folding table stacked with cardboard boxes, and underneath the table a heap of shoes, including what looked like a snowshoe. There was the sickening odor of propane gas, and another of what I guessed was kitty litter that hadn't been changed. The gas worried me. I began to knock more vigorously, and even took off my clog and started banging on the door with the wooden sole. Someone in the apartment across the hall opened his door and looked out.

"Are you one of June's friends?" he said. His tone was vaguely sarcastic.

"I guess so," I said.

"She should be out in a minute," he said. "Just keep banging."

At last the chain was unhitched, and there was June, wrapped in a blanket, her beautiful hair fanning over her shoulders. Her face was bleary with sleep but her eyes were wide open. She seemed surprised to see me, as if she had never asked me to come—really, as if she had never seen me before in her life.

"Come in," she said.

"I'm sorry I'm late," I said, realizing at once how ridiculous that was. I followed her in, and she stood in the center of the messy room and stared around at the clutter as if looking for someplace to put me. She cleared some books from a chair and sat down in it herself. A door clicked open from a room in the back. "Just a minute," June called, and the door clicked shut. She yawned, and pulled a bare arm out from under the blanket, and found a cigarette on the table and lit it. It was the first time I had seen her with a cigarette. Her hand, I noticed, was perfectly steady. She stared at me and let out a stream of smoke.

"I think I need to get a little more sleep," she began. "I was up all night. Don't go. There's food ..." She gestured toward the kitchen. "I'll be up in a while. Not long. I still want to go sailing."

"So do I," I lied. I didn't know if I was angry or hurt or both. Anyway I tried not to show it. She smiled at me weakly and left. For a while I examined the room but there was too much to look at, piles of books and papers, odds and ends, and on the top shelf of the bookcase, sitting all in a row and out of my reach, a bunch of old stuffed animals. On the walls were some charcoal drawings of June, but the likenesses weren't that good and the shading was amateurish. I had been wrong about the kitty litter. There was a dog mess, on a sheaf of newspaper spread out in one corner of the kitchen. It was a small dog. A Pekinese. I found her asleep in a bread basket on a low shelf of the open cupboard. I lifted her up and carried her over to the window and we stood there and looked out at the back of a building exactly like the one we were in. Staring across at its windows, I expected to see the two of us looking back at ourselves. I held the dog close to my breast, like an infant. She pressed her nose against the pane and left a small moist dot on the glass. The window, I saw, was covered with these spots. After a while she started squirming and I lowered her back into her basket.

I opened the refrigerator. There were two ceramic bowls piled high with strawberries, and a glass jar filled with brown water. I unscrewed the lid and sniffed, apprehensive about what I might find. Spiced tea. I poured myself a glass and sat on the floor in the main room with a bowl of strawberries cradled in my lap, pinching the tops off and popping the berries into my mouth one after another. I dropped the green leafy tops back into the bowl. I can't tell you how lonely I felt. I was sitting in a square of sunlight, and when it shifted I inched along with it. Someone was moaning at the back of the house, and gasping. It was impossible to know whether the person who was moaning was the same one who was gasping. Then the telephone rang. It was right at my feet but I didn't pick it up. I let it ring. It rang twelve times. The gasping and moaning continued. My mouth began to sting, from the cold tartness of the berries, but I kept on eating. I held each berry whole in my mouth, sucking the juices out, then pressing it up against the roof of my mouth and crushing it under my tongue. My stomach made wet sloshing noises like a washing machine. I picked up the phone and dialed home, wanting suddenly more than anything to talk with Jack, to tell him what a lousy time I was having and that I wished I hadn't come and that I hoped he would forgive me.

"Forgive you for what?" Jack said.

I didn't know how to respond to that. I sat there in silence. The moaning had ceased but the dog was whimpering. Somehow I had shut the cupboard door and locked her inside. I got up, carrying the phone, and went into the kitchen to let her out. With my free hand I stroked the dog's head, tracing the shape of her broad bony skull with my fingers.

"What's that?" said Jack.

"A dog," I said.

"What do you have in your mouth?"

"A strawberry."

"When are you coming home?"

"I don't know," I said. "Tonight. It's a long drive for nothing."

"Mmmm," Jack said. He would be pressing his lips together, turning them under and holding them shut with his teeth. How familiar he was. He is a gentle man; I have never known another man who does that with his teeth.

"I'll have to be going," I said. "This is costing June a lot of money."

"Mmmm," Jack said. He hung up first. He always guesses when I am waiting for him to hang up, and he never makes me wait too long.

June's lover was tall and olive-skinned and had a mustache almost as thick as a man's. She might have taken some pills. She walked with a swagger, in a bleached demin jacket and jeans and square-toed boots, and she had a mole on her face, in precisely the spot where Marilyn Monroe had one. The effect was freakish. Her name was Faye. I thought to myself, Swarthy Faye. Faye the Pirate. Captain Faye and the Sharks. I saw her as the lead singer in a rock band, dressed in cloak and dagger on a darkened stage in a low-ceilinged room, breathing a song. Her voice would be deep and airy like the sound a bottle makes when you blow into it. I can't remember her actual voice. I don't know that I heard it even once. She stayed close to June, like a body guard, and gave her looks fraught with meaning that I could not decipher.

June seemed confused. I think she had expected me to leave while they were still in bed, at the same time hoping I would stay. I was determined to go sailing. Otherwise, I told myself, why would I have come? She still looked tired, and she had wrapped her hair in a madras scarf so you couldn't see it. She was smoking again. Faye kept the cigarettes in the breast pocket of her jacket, and every time June wanted a smoke she had to reach in and get one.

"You had a telephone call," I said, in voice that was too cheerful. I worked as a receptionist at a hotel in town—that was my receptionist voice.

"Who was it?" asked June, startled.

"No one," I said. "I mean I didn't answer it."

"Thank god," June said. Faye smiled, barely, and at no one in particular. We drank instant coffee black, because the fake cream was stuck like a rock in the bottom of the jar. June bent a spoon, trying to get it out. We all laughed when she held up the bent spoon, then stopped abruptly when it clattered in the sink. There was no mention of a breakfast more substantial than strawberries and coffee. By then, anyway, it was lunch time, sun streaming through the windows. June's arms were golden in the sunlight. I was wondering whether, if June and I had been alone, we would have made pancakes. All at once I remembered the time years ago when, as a teenager, I spent my first night with a boy, on a mattress in the closet of an empty house on some church grounds. In the morning we went to the house of a friend, a motherly girl in an apron, who cooked a batch of pancakes and left the kitchen while we ate them. Thinking of this, I couldn't recall the boy's name. The sole image I had was of his Adam's apple bobbing up and down above my face, the forlorn, boyish shape of the bone with the skin stretched whitely over it. I remembered I told him his balls looked like plums, and how shocked he looked when I said it.

The noon hour stretched on. Then June stood up suddenly and announced it was time to go sailing. We walked the few blocks to the harbor, June chatting on and off about how rich her brother was. His boat was moored at a dock crowded with other boats. There were hordes of people, tying and untying ropes, having just come in or else preparing to go out into the bay, and some who just lounged around in bathing suits as if they had no intention of going anywhere. I have never familiarized myself with the mechanics of sailing and sat on the deck, holding my clogs in my lap while June and Faye passed ropes back and forth and hooked and unhooked things. June disappeared below for a minute, and reappeared with three chilled beers that she passed around. Faye popped the tab off and tossed it right into the water, where it floated. I glanced at June, who shrugged sheepishly, and for a moment there was only the two of us, in the boat that was creaking and bobbing. She made a point of sitting near me while applying some tanning lotion. She had stripped down to her swimsuit. When there was too much lotion left on her hands, she rubbed it into my neck. Her hands were warm. The scent of coconuts rose around us. I didn't know what to do. Faye stared out at the harbor past a string of boats, drinking her beer very fast. Then, when she was finished, she crushed the can with her boot and threw it with perfect aim into the mouth of a trash can on the dock, disappointing me. June clapped, and Faye came to join her, and they started the motor and we were off.

It was slow going. The harbor was jammed. I was struck by the camaraderie of boaters; there was much waving and shouting back and forth. Every few yards we had to stop and sit still while the hot smell of gasoline seared the air. I cringed each time Faye lit June's cigarette, half expecting a blast. Faye wouldn't look at me, but June smiled each time the sun dipped behind a cloud. Suddenly there were clouds, loose black clumps in patches on the hard blue sky, throwing intermittent shadows on the water. You could see, if you looked way into the distance into the bay itself, how the strung sails brightened and then vanished and then brightened again as they traveled through light and darkness.

"Jack would have liked this," I said.

"You should have brought him along," said June.

"You should have told me to," I said. Faye took June's hand and placed her own long-boned hand on top of it. They nuzzled and sighed.

At the lip of the bay the coast guard stopped us. There was a man with a megaphone. A storm was approaching. Overhead the clouds had clumped and there was thunder far off. The air had grown thick and electric. A few tendrils of hair had escaped from June's scarf; they glowed like filaments. Goose bumps appeared on our arms, but there was nothing to be frightened of as long as we turned back. I was relieved. The ocean looked crazy. We hadn't even put up our sails. The city was still in sunlight, but we knew it wouldn't last. We shared another beer, not bothering to speak above the churn of the motors. Docked, we covered the boat with a tarpaulin and walked home as the rain started falling. I have never seen such large drops of rain, like grapes. June caught some in her mouth, and then Faye took her jacket off and lifted it over our heads. More than once I stepped out of my clog and they waited for me without turning around. We all smelled by the time we got home. Salt and sweat. The apartment was stifling and so dark we were blinded. June sniffed. "I've got to change that newspaper," she said. "Poor Phyllis." Then she turned to me and touched me very lightly on the wrist. "Faye and I are taking a shower," she said.

I kissed Phyllis good-bye and grabbed a handful of strawberries and left. For a while I sat in the car and waited for the rain to let up, chewing slowly to ward off my hunger. For days, I felt, I had been eating nothing else, like someone lost in a forest. I just wanted to get home. On the highway I took a wrong turn. They had to turn me around at a toll booth, stopping traffic so I could cut across the lanes.

Jack wasn't home when I got there. He had been busy; the bed was stacked with laundry. The windows were open, and the floor was streaked with rain. It was the season of mildew, and I could smell it on the towel as I wiped the perspiration from my face. I was tired, too tired to undress. I fell among the fresh-washed clothes and slept.

Later that night, Jack came home. He smelled like soap. I have never asked him where he was and he has never told me. At the time I was too sick to care. My throat and tongue were parched, and my limbs ached dully. He helped me out of my clothes and fed me water and aspirin. He dampened a washcloth and held it briefly to my face, which he told me was swollen. My lips felt swollen and tasted of brine. I refused to eat. Jack brought me hot cups of broth, which cooled before I touched them.

"What could it be?" he said, on the second day, when I was feeling a little better. I was sitting up in bed, just sitting, still dazed, doing nothing.

"Strawberries," I said. "Look at this rash. What else could it be?"

"Mmmm," Jack said. He was brushing my hair, a lock at a time. His strokes were even and gentle. That was when we turned the television on, and Ronald Reagan said what he said, and Jack threw the brush and hit him in the face and broke it. It fell to the floor in two pieces. I don't remember the rest of the news, if there was any. We just sat very close. I think I told him about the man in the Winnebago, just then remembering him. Then we both went to sleep. Ten years have gone by, and it is suddenly the season, and believe me when I say I haven't touched another strawberry since.

Engagements

Jeffrey and I agreed four years ago that if we ever have a baby we'll get married without a word, with no second thoughts and little ceremony, just a case of San Miguel Dark and a few hastily scribbled invitations. If we don't make a big deal of it, we said, nobody else will. There will be no T-shirts printed with our names, no weeping, and not too many flowers. Of course I ponder, in private, as I am certain he must also, the question: why marry for the baby if not for ourselves? What difference could it make to a child? It is a troublesome question, fragile as crystal and as cold to the touch.

I've learned to be careful with questions. Joanne, for instance, who lived across the street from us before we moved and wears her white uniform even on off hours, thinks I am pushy or rude. Tactless. I know this because her husband, who used to smile whenever he saw me, no longer did. He no longer waved when I passed. He looked the other way or past me at the tops of trees or at my feet. I spoke to Joanne only twice. The first time, she was kneeling in her yard, prying weeds from between the bricks in their front walk. I thought she might like to know that her skirt was up around her hips but when she saw me coming she stood up and straightened it out and smiled, so instead I asked her what it was like to be a nurse. She said she wasn't a nurse but a nurse's aide, that the patients were senile and usually got her down, that she was tired of lugging bedpans and changing bibs, that the TVs blast incessantly but there are flowers everywhere. She seemed startled that I had asked and went on to explain, in detail, the callousness of the doctors. She said more often than not they don't know what they're doing, that they are heartless bastards, that people are always dying.

The next time I saw her I invited her over for a cup of tea. She is plump and cheerful and efficient; when I spilled the whole bowlful of sugar she whisked it away with a paper towel while I stood cursing. As soon as we were seated on the front porch, drinking our tea, I asked her why she got married. She shivered a bit and pulled an old pink sweater tighter around her, but this could have been the chill in the air. It was autumn. She said quite abruptly that she was in love with Richard. Richard is her husband.

"But why bother to get married?" I pressed. "What's the point?"

"It's not a bother. I'm proud to be his wife."

We didn't say much after that. I counted the leaves that fell as we sat there. Five leaves. She was staring across the street at her house, which was a large house for a childless couple.

"Are you going to have a family?" I asked.

"Of course. Of course we're going to."

She left when her glass was still half full.

Whenever I ask Jeffrey whether or not I am beautiful he compares my cheekbones to those of an Indian woman whose picture he has pasted to the refrigerator. She is a Sioux, standing in a wheat field, cradling a bundle of it in her arms. Her eyes are wide and wet-looking. Her face is pained. Her hair, which falls across her chest, is coiled like rope. My cheekbones, Jeffrey tells me, could very well be hers.

"But she looks like her IBM is plummeting," I say unfairly. "What on earth do you see in her?"

"She's suffering," he says. "She's lost her mate." From this I understand that he thinks he knows everything about her, that he has imagined making love to her. When he talks this way he stares at the ceiling while one corner of his mouth twitches and turns up as if he is trying not to laugh. I don't know if he takes himself seriously.

"But is *she* beautiful?"

"Come to think of it," he says, "the shape of her face"—tracing the line from eye to chin with the eraser of his pencil— "the general effect. It could very well be yours."

It's like ordering tea in a restaurant and getting a little ceramic pot filled with steamy water and a teacup with a Lipton tea bag inside. You never get quite what you're after.

Jeffrey is thirty-three. I am twenty-seven. He is a lawyer with a downtown firm, I am part-owner of the bookstore, and we have just moved into this house, this tall brick house which is a step up from anything else we've lived in because it has a fenced back yard and several small leaded windows. It was amazing luck, really, this house. We had gone for a drive in Jeffrey's MG. It was the first real spring day: the forsythia suddenly blooming, the buds on the magnolias beginning to swell, the streets lined with joggers. Jeffrey had put on his driving cap, a jaunty tweed he inherited from his father and wears only on rare occasions, then he'd picked a sprig of forsythia and stuck it in my hair.

"There," he said, stepping back to look at me. "We're both suitably out of character."

We drove around for an hour and then we saw the house. One of the two front doors was open and a man wearing white overalls was painting it scarlet to match the other. The windows, three on each side, are arranged symmetrically and have scarlet shutters. There is a chimney on either side and a neat row of ivy grows straight up the middle, dividing the whole house into two perfect halves.

"How tacky," we both said.

On the front lawn was a sign which read FOR SALE and beneath that in smaller letters, OR RENT. We stopped. When the man saw us he put down the brush and wiped his face, leaving a smudge of paint the size of a strawberry. He said, "Pets and children welcome," and showed us the house. It had arched doorways leading from one room to another, a set of steps which made a right-angle turn, a bathroom papered with the kind of print you usually see on flannel nightgowns, a sunroom whose sills were spotted with leaves, and a fireplace with a hearth. There was an old air hockey table with two broken legs and a chipped enamel stepping stool in the kitchen. The kitchen had blue tiles on the walls and was clean and provincial-looking. I signed the lease and Jeffrey made out a check for the security deposit and the first month's rent.

Before we left, the man took us out back and showed us the yard, proudly, as if it were something he had invented. The previous tenants had left a sandbox and one lawn chair and a swing set. He let me give the swing a trial push and took a whole fistful of sand from the sandbox to let it sift through his fingers while we watched. He showed us the vine which had spread in all directions on the back fence. It's rose, he said. Yellow rose. There is azalea too, and a clump of long tapered leaves he told us was iris. In August there are lots of bees, he said, but they stick to the flowers and don't bother a soul.

On our lease it is stated quite clearly that we have the option to buy, that any money we've spent toward rent would go automatically toward purchase should we decide ... The print is so small we have to read it with a magnifying glass from Jeffrey's *Oxford English Dictionary*. Perhaps that is what makes the possibility of buying seem so remote that we barely discuss it, the thought of ownership becoming like so many words in the dictionary. It is obsolete. It is not part of our vocabularly.

This house, we agree, is very nearly perfect. Nothing falters or slips, shatters or cracks. There are no cobwebs, no rust under the sinks, no spiders, nothing but an occasional ladybug or a moth with exquisite wings. It's the type of house you'd want to live in for the rest of your life if you wanted to live in one house for the rest of your life. Jeffrey and I have been living together for four years and we've moved three times. It's something we do well together. We wrap things in newspaper— cups, saucers, forks, spoons. We put them in boxes. We roll whole sheets of comics into balls and stuff them in the spaces. We tape the boxes shut. We write our names on them. We put them in my car and drive them across town to our new house. Our new house is always across town. South to north. North to west. West to east. I think of northwest, southeast, north-northeast. The possibilities are endless.

The other side of the house is owned by Katy and Sam. They

are younger than we are and have a child, a little girl named Sharry. Sharry wears tiny red boxer shorts and a T-shirt with rabbits on it. The rabbits are copulating. She asked us several times, as we carted our furniture past her and into the house, if we had a birdbath. "It's her favorite word," Katy explained. "She's never even seen one." Katy is quite pregnant again and spends most of her time sitting on the front porch with her legs propped on pillows, reading or weaving on a table loom. She has a full face and thick dark hair and Jeffrey says she is the most beatific thing he's ever seen. Sam is an economics professor at a local college we had never heard of. He doesn't wear a shirt but keeps a red bandanna wrapped around his head. He is always in the back yard, "keeping it in shape." I get tired just watching him, pruning the bushes and painting the gutters and building things. He built a playhouse for Sharry, a stone wall with a barbecue built into it, and a tiny brick patio hedged with pansies. There is a neat little fence between our yard and theirs. Sam apologized for it the very first time we met him. He said he built it just for something to do and if we wanted he would take it down.

Our street, like all others on this side of the park, is lined with magnolia and cherry trees; the grass underneath is thick with violets; the lawns are spotted with dandelions and cut haphazardly at best. It is pleasant at this time of year. Balls roll into the streets and children bounce after them. Tricycles rattle on the sidewalks at early morning and at dusk. On weekends the smell of barbecue floats into our rooms like an invitation. Today, because it is Sunday, Jeffrey dons the chef's apron I bought him as a joke and sets bottle after bottle before him on the table to concoct, his wrists precise as a magician's, the marinade I cannot duplicate. He cuts, with the cleaver he sharpens assiduously on the first Sunday of every other month, the filet into eight perfect cubes and drops them one by one into the marinade. Then he licks his fingers and starts on the vegetables—bell pepper, onion, tomato, all sliced into quarters and arranged geometrically by color on the cutting board, like a mosaic. Finally he peels four tiny new potatoes to be popped on the end of each skewer after all else has been speared, to keep everything in place.

There is a picture of a kangaroo on the apron I bought him. The kangaroo has a pocket from which poke the heads of various ladles and wooden spoons. Jeffrey looks young and foolish in the apron; I don't know if he knows I bought it as a joke. Cooking, he said to me once, is part of the routine of making life seem more important than it is; it must be perfected.

Before cooking we go for a walk on the island of green in the center of the road, under a tunnel of magnolias. The flowers came all at once five days ago; they are luminous and pink and full. "I could stand here forever," I say, "just looking at them." Jeffrey says no, if you stand there long enough you'll see them wither and drop. He has that half-smile on his face. "Just show me one thing," he says, squeezing my breast, "that won't wither and drop."

In the distance someone is bouncing a ball and singing the alphabet song. A my name is Alma and I live in Alabama and my husband's name is ... "That's why people have kids," I say suddenly. "You don't see it happen."

We eat dinner on the back steps, fending off mosquitoes as evening settles around us and the swing set darkens. Next door on either side the children have quieted and all we can hear is the whisper of paper plates.

"All right," says Jeffrey. "So you've convinced me. Now what?"

"Now what what?"

"What do we call it? Where will it sleep? When do we do it?"

"Do you love me?"

He taps a plastic fork against his teeth. "Explain the term," he says. "Define it."

Jeffrey is a better cook than I am. Every Sunday the marinade is slightly different. This is, I am certain, by design.

My parents first met him five years ago when they flew to the city for a visit. The four of us had dinner in a seafood restaurant. My mother in a beach hat, for atmosphere. Jeffrey ordered stuffed crab and asparagus spears, a civilized meal. The stuffed crab was all stuff and no crab and Jeffrey called the waiter to the table, silently, with one raised finger. "Did you forget the crab?" he asked innocently, and proceeded to pick at the food with his fork, lifting out morsels of breadcrumb and celery until nothing was left. He prodded the shell with a knife, poking it into the hollows. "It's really quite a lovely shell," he said. "Where's the crab?"

"Would you care to see the manager?" The waiter peered at the plate, eyebrows raised. Our food was getting cold.

"No, thank you," said Jeffrey. "I'd rather see the crab."

The waiter left and returned with a plate of steaming crab meat. He spooned it into the shell and sprinkled it with the breadcrumbs and celery. "Ah yes," Jeffrey said. My father winked at me from across the table. Later he pulled me aside. "Your Jeffrey will make a fine lawyer," he said, slapping me hard on the back.

So Jeffrey makes it look like my idea, the baby. When he carts three boxes of books upstairs to the sunroom I say no, we'll leave the sunroom empty, furnish it for Cris, when he or she is born. He feigns a surprised acquiescence; just yesterday he said the sunroom was the ideal room for a child, all those windows laced with ivy. Of course we are careful to say "he or she." Katy calls her unborn child John, patting her belly each time she says it. It makes me terribly uncomfortable. I show her the house when most everything is in place. She says she wants to see what it's like, a mirror image of her own house. "Like Alice in Wonderland," she says. "Through the looking glass." When we come to the sunroom I have to tell her we're planning to use it as our library as soon as we get the shelves built. We don't want anyone to know about Cris until they can see for themselves.

The sunroom has black and white tiles on its floor, and white walls with black trim around the windows. At midnight it glows like the inside of a shell, like a pearl, with a mute pale light. "It seems only fair that Cris should be conceived in his or her room," says Jeffrey one night. We spread our big Mexican blanket on the floor, throw in two pillows, and take a bottle of liqueur from the nightstand in the bedroom. This goes on for four nights; on the fifth day my body is covered with small yellow bruises and I am certain my hips have been flattened like two weathered stones. My period starts early. Jeffrey is disappointed. He says, "How can that be?" and smiles his half-smile as we fold up the blanket. We like to fold it just right, taking hold of the corners and standing at blanket's length from one another, making sure the edges meet. It is something like a dance, our folding the blanket, ceremoniously, as if there were something inside.

More and more often I feel myself drawn to the porch, to Katy. She seems in perpetual repose and I wonder if this is her nature or her pregnancy. She wears those cotton maternity shifts with floral designs or stripes or polka dots. There is often a band of lace at the neck, and puffed sleeves similarly trimmed. The shifts have pockets shaped like hearts or apples; Sharry is always running up and sticking her hands in them, pulling out a bit of yarn, a cookie, a crayon. Katy fills the pockets in the morning and by evening, she tells me, they're empty. When the sun hits she holds a reflector to her collarbone, serene and motionless as a lily pad.

I try to imagine what it is like, carrying a baby. Looking at Katy doesn't help much because we're so unlike. Flesh covers her like a soft pink quilt. I am angular and hard, my hips are sharp and narrow. Jeffrey is concerned: will there be room in there? He says he can see right through to my bones, he can see exactly how I'm put together.

The baby, I hope, will change all that. People say that faces change, that they blossom into a kind of calm, like Katy's face. A woman who works the cash register at Woolworth's claims she can guess the sex of an unborn child simply by looking at the mother's face. "It's a boy," she told Katy. "When it's a boy the face has more secrets."

Sometimes Katy offers me a piece of fruit or cheese and today I mix two glasses of ice tea before going out to the porch. She tells me about sun tea. You put a couple of tea bags in a jar of water and then you set it in the sun. The jar gets warm, the water turns golden, in a day or two you have it.

"Tea," she says. "A miracle."

She scans the lawn, a hand above her eyes. Sharry has stepped to the edge of the sidewalk and places one foot on the pavement. A car speeds past; she sways like a flower, hair fanning out from her head. What is she thinking? Suddenly there is Katy, lifting her up, slapping her backside, sending her onto the porch. Sharry laughs, delighted with adventure. When Katy sits down sweat gleams on her hairline, like mercury.

Soon she is weaving, her hands calm and measured. She's making a blanket for John. Pale blue. Look closely and you can see the shapes of tiny houses woven into the wool. Rows and rows of them. "Run your hand along it," she tells me. She pushes the weft back and forth. "You can feel them, like Braille."

Jeffrey pokes fun of the fact that I sit here. He says imitating Katy won't make me pregnant. Katy is utterly composed; even her feet propped up on the porch railing look as if they belong there. It is disconcerting at times, watching her. I look at the covers of her books. There are always pictures of women, and the women are always running.

It is August suddenly, and Cris is as yet unconceived. Of course this is not unusual, people have waited years, but we are beginning to wonder. Perhaps it is something in ourselves, keeping it from happening? We get along reasonably, peaceably as the parts of a dining room set. We like to buy exotic liqueurs—peach, apricot, anise—and drink them from wine glasses after dark. We make love often and in various places: the bathtub, the stairwell, the back porch at midnight. Neither one of us cries out. Our love is spontaneous and refreshing as a glass of lemonade. After, we lie side by side and read. It is something we do well together, reading. Jeffrey holds the book. I turn the pages. The topics vary—primitive peoples, foreign countries, wars, paintings. Jeffrey likes to say that we're engaged in something useful, that we're learning about the world, but at parties he is known to come out with statements like "There is a man who is so in love with the whale he is studying that he named her Ella and sleeps every night in a rowboat in her tank." This starts everyone talking. Personally I'm not concerned with the history of jazz or the private lives of politicians or the ways in which meteors fall. It has always been enough to know that such things exist, that there are histories, private lives, that things fall. If anything, it is consoling to know that Jeffrey and I will cultivate a common knowledge, consoling to read a passage he is reading, that there is this link between us.

Tonight we are reading *An Analysis of Children's Drawings.* "You can learn things," said Jeffrey, handing me the book, "by looking at their pictures." We examine them closely, as if we were in a museum. The pictures seem ordinary and harmless—a house with flowers bursting from a window box, a dog, a cat, a tree with apples on it. The people have eyes set high on their foreheads, and most of them are smiling. But there are clues, the book instructs. Hands, for instance. "The child who consistently draws large hands shows a potential for violence. Small hands indicate a feeling of insecurity." It goes on. "This drawing of a woman with small pointed breasts betrays the unloved, reproachful child. Note, also, that the woman's hands are hidden behind her back."

"You have small pointed breasts," says Jeffrey.

"You have large hands," I tell him. He holds them up, flexing his fingers. We flip through the rest of the book. In most of the drawings the sky is a thin strip of blue at the top of the page and the clouds, scalloped and cheerful, have sunk below it. For the first time in two and a half months we forego our liqueurs. We leave the wine glasses untouched, turn away from each other, and sleep. The wine glasses are the plastic kind with the removable stem. Jeffrey bought a whole bag of them once. We've used the same two over and over. It's one of our games, to see how long they'll last.

It's a flat hot Sunday, everything buzzing—hedge pruners, lawn mowers, transistor radios. Bees buzz in and out of windows and the air itself hums as if struggling to come to life. Sam is strumming a guitar, his bandanna dark with sweat. Katy fills a laundry tub with water, lifts Sharry by the armpits, and dips her into it, first one foot, then the other. Water splashes around the two of them. There's a platter of chicken in the refrigerator, and some gazpacho, featured in the recipe segment of today's paper, which Katy insisted on making. "I've got to have it," she said, and sent Sam to the yard for tomatoes.

Katy, whose belly startled me this morning when I saw her in her suit, is delighting more than ever in the final stages of her pregnancy. She makes us lay our ears against her belly to hear the baby's heart because, she says, she can't hear it herself. Jeffrey assures her it's beating. "Thump-thump. Thump-thump," he says. I don't tell them it reminds me of the ocean in the conch shell; put your ear to a shell and hear your own blood breaking like waves.

Later, gazpacho and chicken. Jeffrey finds the wishbone and cleans it with his teeth. He rubs it with a napkin and turns it in the light until it gleams and then he beckons Sharry to his side and grins like a father.

"This is a wishbone," he explains. "You shut your eyes and make a wish and then you grab hold of it and pull."

Sharry shuts her eyes, squeezes them tight. Jeffrey cracks the bone a little in her favor and then they play. He grits his teeth. The bone snaps.

"You won, old girl," says Jeffrey. "What was your wish?"

Sharry blinks at him and at the splintered bone. She starts to cry. "What's a wish?" she says.

Later we look it up in the *Oxford English Dictionary.* "A wish," I read aloud, "is the expression of an unrealized or un-realizable desire."

"That leaves the problem of desire," says Jeffrey. "How can you teach them anything?"

We convert the sunroom into a library of sorts, with rows of books under the windows and a reading lamp next to an armchair. We spend a pleasant morning taking the books from their boxes, dusting them off, and arranging them by subject on their shelves. "It's perfect," says Jeffrey, surveying the room. We've always wanted a library. It's quite a relief, now that the house is complete. We bought cedar planks and cinder blocks at the lumber yard. The cedar has a sharp clean scent. It fills the air.

We still have our Sunday barbecues but it's chillier each week. The first leaves are falling. Sam and Katy's fireplace is filling up with leaves. We see them scattered on the road, one here, one there. Jeffrey comments that the street will be unbearably bleak in winter. "I don't know if I can take it," he says from the window. "All those empty trees." Sometimes I see him watching other women—the way they walk, the slope of their necks, the cast of their eyes. At night, even after he's read the paper, he turns on the television news to watch, I am certain, a particular anchorwoman whose hands flit about on the paper as she speaks, nervous as butterflies. She won't last long. Every so often I point this out to him. I say, "Would you like me more if I moved my hands too when I spoke, like this?" He shrugs when I say this and pats my hand. But when I go out back to look at the flowers he follows, a hand on my back. The irises never came up. There is sweet pea, and tiny sprigs of mint with purple flowers. "Mint is the only plant with a square stem," I say to Jeffrey. It is something we read months ago. The roses bloomed late and will last into September. They have a queer waxy sheen and I touch them lightly with the very tips of my fingers, the way you touch the flowers on the tables in restaurants to see if they're real.

Katy had a boy and he cries all night so we've taken to turning on the radio before we go to sleep. This is something we've never done before. Every other night we change the station. We sleep with our ears to the speakers. We are learning about different kinds of music.

Paradise

On the bed at Joanie's is a floral quilt I'd never noticed; the antique petals of the giant roses, filmy as ghosts, have faded into their creamy background. Her wallpaper is faded as well but adorned with ferns arranged in broad, unfernlike clusters, like the fanned tops of palm trees, and on the rug that the land-lord left behind is a border of plump white blossoms of inde-terminate species, with dense, leafy bracts and vivid yellow cones at their centers.

The room is close and chaotic in a way that I have come to expect of Joanie herself, but today the effect is subdued; a floor fan ticks rhythmically in a corner and the air spins lazily around us. Joanie is wearing her floral skirt and an airy blouse whose short, generous sleeves undulate in the fan's current. She looks fragrant and cool, weightless as a dandelion seed. In her lap lies a white plastic comb whose tapered handle she strokes au-tomatically. She keeps looking at the flowers I brought her, looking and then glancing away and then glancing back, as if carnations were magical and might suddenly lapse into the pattern on the quilt and become unreal.

I've known Joanie five years, but haven't seen her since May, six weeks ago when Tim and I were married. Tim was Joanie's lover first. I met him in this very room in February, and it didn't take long for any of us to figure out what was happening. But Joanie is proud, and she and I are still friends. Even so I can't imagine why I ever thought of bringing her flowers. I don't know if the colors are dyed or natural. The lady in the shop couldn't say and was embarrassed by the colors I chose, peach and mauve, with one bright, blood-red flower off-center among the others. I took a long time choosing these colors, adding and subtracting carnations like someone demonstrating a mathematical equation, all the while standing bare-legged in the blast of icy air from the open cooler. I thrust the bouquet through the neck of an empty Gallo burgundy jug I'd brought along in my shopping bag. At Joanie's, I filled the jug with water from the tap. The sink was choked with dishes and pots and pans that had to be moved out of the way. When Joanie came to watch, we stood side by side till the water gushed out from the mouth of the bottle, spraying us.

Joanie is small but graceful, with strong slender bones and a high, arched neck; her body gives one the impression of being braver than it might actually be. Circling one wrist is a heavy, crudely cut, man's watchband. Ordinarily her features are sturdy and cool, blunt and forthcoming. But she doesn't want to talk about herself and asks about our trip. Tim and I honeymooned on an island in the British Virgins. The place was embarrassing, a volcanic countryside lush with sugarcane, palms, poverty, and garbage. Our hotel smelled musty and sat on an isolated stretch of beach spotted with oil. Next door, on some mudflats, lived a colony of pigs among discarded kitchen appliances. A land crab inhabited our closet; we heard it scuttling all night between the straps of our sandals.

We had a wonderful time. We swam naked, and in the evenings drove rusted go-carts around a paved track. We ate crawfish that the local boys gathered, and bought T-shirts from women in flapping skirts. I had my hair done in corn rows one day on the beach. The woman thanked me when I'd paid her, then pointed out over the sea to where some clouds had sunk. It rained every day far out on the water. Tim and I stayed close together, like mating fish. In May, when we were married, we were certain being married couldn't make any difference. But somehow, I find myself saying to Joanie, things have changed. We grew closer on that island, isolated, as if the world didn't matter, as if nothing mattered.

"I began to worry we were living such an ordinary life, but not anymore," I say blithely. "It doesn't bother us, we're so bourgeois, that's our big joke."

And on and on, until finally there's silence and Joanie finds a cigarette and says, "Tim once told me he wanted to get into *politics.*"

She laughs, puts the cigarette to her lips, and strikes a match, but the match won't flare—it's too damp or old, it keeps snapping and fizzling. She climbs from her chair in search of another, finding one at last in a pottery bowl on the bookcase. By then she has misplaced the cigarette, and circles the room with the matches in hand, one already disengaged and waiting to be struck. There's a half-empty pack on the table near my jug of gaudy flowers, but she won't give up, she wants the original cigarette.

Later we go walking in the hot midwestern air. Joanie pauses to window shop, as soon as we get past the seminary to some stores, but eventually we cut through the alley to the parking lot where our friend Mary lives. It seems inevitable that we should gravitate toward Mary's, as if seeking shared ground. The carved front porch of Mary's relic of a house overhangs the pavement. Her building was condemned until she bought it several years ago with government help and put the floors back in. Fake Spanish tile. She always says she prefers a wood floor over a Spanish one, but since there's no such thing as fake wood she settled for the fake tile.

The doorways are arched and go nicely with the tile, but the kitchen is a cubbyhole. Mary cooks only for herself, anyway. She's our mothers' age. When I met her and ran into people who knew her, I kept hearing what a stoic she was, such a proud woman, how brave in the face of things.

"What things?" I asked. But nobody knew. Mary's life is a secret, even from us, who sit gabbing with her till two in the morning, watching her mix drinks. She's a lady, really. I like to look at the soaps in her bathroom—carved roses, tiny lemons and plums. She comes from Maine. All night her phone rings and it's someone from Maine she's been thinking of, she's been meaning to call, she wrote a letter but never sent it. All of this is always true. On the floor in her living room is a bronze nude that has turned green. Mary's amethyst sunglasses perch on the nude's nose. I have a theory that Mary has a son in jail in Turkey, or a dead lover somewhere, or some family heirlooms buried near a gas station in Poland. Some tragedy. She hinted once that she had business abroad but could not afford to get there. On her back landing, through a door leading out from the tiny kitchen, sits a parrot in a cage. The parrot says one word. Cecil.

"Cecil is the goddamn psychiatrist that finally got the hell out of my life," Mary said once. I retold this to the people who asked about her past, but everyone had already heard it.

Mary serves rum and Coke when we get there. She always hops up the minute you show up at the door, and before you know it there's a glass of something in your hand and a stained straw coaster on the table in front of you. Also the ashtrays get passed around, and maybe some grapes, and then the cat makes its way onto everyone's lap, purring steadily.

"Written me any poems lately?" Mary asks Joanie.

"Not really."

"Oh sure." Mary digs around in the chair cushions for a minute, finds her eyeglasses, and puts them on. She takes them off again, wipes the lenses on her skirt hem, and puts them back on. "I can't find a goddamn good poetry book anywhere," she says loudly. "They're all boring trash. I can't get into anything. I want a good humid poem."

"Try James Dickey," I suggest.

"I've read James Dickey. I love James Dickey."

"Try Roethke. He's got some humid ones. Lots of mud."

"I want bodies. I can't explain what I want. I don't know what I want. Anyway this thing sure doesn't have it."

She slaps the cover of a giant library book, and then suggests a picnic for Saturday. "Maybe a picnic will get this slug of a summer moving," she says, and keeps slapping the book methodically. The room is piled with books and shoes—books under the furniture, shoes on top of the furniture, shoes on the porch, books in the bathroom. You could traverse the place from book to shoe, like crossing a stream on rocks. But Mary is barefoot. She was painting her toenails when we arrived. The nail polish sits on the table, and only four of her toes have been painted. She won't do it in our presence. She will wait for us to go.

"You two," she says finally, and lets her book slide catlike from the arm of her chair. "Well, well, well."

Saturday is warm and cloudless, alright for a picnic if you know a shady spot with a breeze. Mary says she knows one and we set off across the playing fields carrying our shopping bags and baskets. We are all wearing skirts, and Mary stuck a rose in her hair. She bought two bottles of retsina and a large jar of sour Greek olives and some tangerines. I made cookies and a bowl of Tim's favorite potato salad. Joanie fried some chicken. Her skirt smells of cooking oil, but she looks dignified as usual. At the picnic spot, where there is no shade to speak of, she comments skeptically and plops herself down. Mary insists it was shaded the last time. She remembers vividly a cool, breezy carpet of unmown grass beneath a circle of spruce trees. But the seminary has since converted the field to an athletic complex, and we sit ourselves down near a dirt running trail between some parallel bars and a balance beam. Behind us spreads the soccer field and track, and to the left the trail vanishes among tall weeds and thistles. Runners sprint past us on the brittle grass, sweat flying. They all nod at our picnic. Mary brought a checkered cloth and we sit lanquidly around it on matching napkins.

"What in god's name is that man doing?" says Mary after a while. She points with her chicken wing across the field to a man doing jumping jacks. From this distance he appears tiny and mechanical, like a windup toy.

"I wonder how much of a hunk he is," she continues. "What do you say, Joanie?"

Joanie squints and says nothing, but I say I don't like his kelly green shorts.

"I didn't ask you," says Mary after a while. "You're still on your honeymoon."

I shrug and say it's true. Mary says she doesn't blame me anyway because Tim has such good taste in potato salad. Joanie snorts and says that *her* potato salad is better than mine. She eats an olive and rolls the pit around in her mouth before spitting it into her palm. Soon the man in the kelly green shorts approaches, and stops at the chin-up bar that in the harsh sun is like a beam from a raygun. Up he goes, and down, and up again, slow as can be with the sweat rolling out of his armpits and the three of us gazing, perched in our skirts on our three checkered napkins, just now feeling the heat. Around his body moves a vapor like the undulating waves above a surface of asphalt, so we watch as if waiting for him to dissolve.

"Drink up," Mary orders, filling our cups with retsina. "This place is no Garden of Eden, I suppose."

She leans back on her elbows and shuts her eyes. Pretty soon we are all three doing this, leaning with our faces into the hard sun, sipping warm beer and bitter retsina, staying quiet. The retsina, in flowered paper cups with cut-out handles, is impossible to swallow. I dump mine in the grass when no one's looking, and fill the cup with froth from my bottle of beer. Every so often some man jogs past, and we offer cookies and forkfuls of potato salad. Then we fall silent again, and that is how the afternoon goes by, like a slow-moving cloud, filmy and out of reach. Joanie tells me I look like a health food ad, my hair fanning out against a backdrop of sky. Then the sun starts to drop and we start packing up, gathering paper cups and cigarette butts and tossing them into a shopping bag along with Mary's eyeglass case and the jar of olives. She offered one to every jogger that went by, but only one accepted. He said he needed some salt. He had a dog and the dog looked thirsty so she gave it a plateful of beer.

"That guy was okay," she comments now. "That guy I gave the olive to with the dog."

"He's taken," says Joanie. "He's a priest."

"I didn't say I wanted to marry him," says Mary, kicking on her sandals. We set off across the field together, between the goal posts on the soccer field.

"We could do this again," I say when we've reached the parking lot, but then I step on a rock and the salad bowl slides from my arms and lands upside down on the pavement. Everyone watches as I pick it up. There's a lopsided yellow mound of potato salad with a fly already buzzing at the edge of it.

"Oh god," I moan. "Poor Tim."

"Come on," Mary calls. "Don't worry your pretty head about Tim."

She's drunk. Just a little. There's an edge to her voice that I've heard all along and not, until just now, taken to heart. Anger. Already at the threshold, she's got the screen door propped against her legs, and the picnic basket wedged between her elbow and hip, and one hand in her pocket feeling for keys, and one hand in the air for balance.

The Anniversary

It is a Friday evening, far too hot for early September. The humidity has been building since noon, and everyone seems pleased with the rainy forecast for the weekend. They talk of rain as if it were a loved one coming home after an absence. Of course the air conditioning is out; Martha dreads the moment when the conductor calls her stop and she'll have to stand up, yanking the backs of her thighs from the vinyl seat like two Band-Aids torn from a wound. She is wearing her tennis dress, not what she usually wears on the LIRR but she had planned a game with Gloria after work. Gloria hadn't shown up. Martha dropped her dime in the club phone, calling. Her hands were trembling. She phoned Gloria's office, but nobody answered. Then she phoned Gloria's home, but her daughter picked up the phone, so Martha kept silent, not wanting to worry her. Maybe something has happened to Gloria. Maybe Gloria is lying on a subway platform. More likely Gloria stopped for a drink and forgot their date, which is just as well because it's too hot for tennis. Martha is glad for an excuse to wear her tennis dress home on the train, instead of her suit and stockings and high-heeled shoes. She is comfortable in her tennis shoes, her bare ankles, her bare arms. The tennis dress is appliquéd with daisies.

When the conductor calls out Hicksville she shuts her eyes. An ancient habit. Six years ago Tom divorced her and moved to Hicksville with a girl who played the piano. The girl was twenty-two, and Martha has never been given the satisfaction of seeing her. Still, when she imagines her, she sees her from behind, seated upright on a piano bench, her hair swept up and fastened with a wicker clip, the pale floral folds of her skirt falling nearly to the floor, her long fingers dancing on the ivory keys. She must have long fingers if she plays the piano. She is still twenty-two, still playing Elton John. The two of them live in a tiny house, one of those identical houses you see from the tracks in Hicksville. The houses are gracious and have parlors in them. Tom drinks scotch; a decanter is filled with the amber liquid. Martha doesn't know which house is theirs, but she is certain it is one of those houses that line the tracks. They are all alike. It doesn't matter which is theirs. Frequently, above the screech and whine of the train, she hears the faint sweet cadence of notes being struck on a piano.

"Must be a hundred degrees on this train," says a young woman sitting next to her. She is sweating and reading a newspaper and she smells of deodorant. Martha is always glad when a woman sits near her instead of a man. Once on this same train, years ago as a newlywed, she dropped her handkerchief in the lap of a man who was sleeping. It was a hot evening, like this one, but in June when she knew she was pregnant, and she wiped the sweat from her face and somehow let go of the handkerchief so it floated to the man's crotch. She couldn't bring herself to pick it up. She remembers staring at it nervously from the corner of her eye. When he wakes up, she told herself, I'll say, "Excuse me but I seem to have dropped my handkerchief." She rehearsed the phrase a million times. "Excuse me but I seem to have dropped my handkerchief," with a discreet tilt of her head toward his lap. But then he grunted in his sleep and tucked in his shirttails. He tucked the handkerchief right into his pants so only a lacy corner remained visible over the belt.

She felt guilty about that for years. She had a vision of the man going home to his wife, chatting with her in the bedroom while he undressed, first his sweaty shirt, then his pants, then the handkerchief falling to the floor at his feet. How could he explain? Martha imagines them going through life, their marriage irreparably altered, a bitter air of puzzlement between them. She wonders what became of her handkerchief. Lately, thinking about it, she finds herself laughing. The laughter is deep in her belly but genuine. She wonders how something that once seemed so cruel has turned funny. She imagines she has grown full of spite.

Shifting in her seat, Martha edges toward the window and crosses her legs so the open newspaper no longer brushes against them. She wishes it were winter. In winter, at dusk, the view from the train is not nearly so dim. There is snow and the light hits it, and maybe there are snowflakes whirling and falling, fine dry flakes so the air is filmy and white. She would get home, start a fire, sit with a book and a glass of wine until she felt hungry or sleepy. She is proud of the fireplace. They both were proud of the fireplace when they bought the house; set into the wall between the living and dining rooms, it opens onto both. It is the saving grace of the house, which is split-level and ordinary, part of a development in which the houses are mirror images of one another. When they purchased the lot, they requested a house in which the kitchen and garage faced south, the bedrooms north. The builder mixed up. He built the house backward, so the kitchen faces north; when you walk in, the stove and sink are on the left. She felt turned around, misplaced, as if she were cooking in somebody else's kitchen. The open fireplace made everything better. When Tom moved out, she made a point of building herself a fire every night when it was cool, and eating dinner on the couch while her son sat close by on the floor, his salad plate clinking on the slate of the hearth. She looked past him through the flames at the shadows moving on the pine-paneled walls of the dining room, and asked about his day. She likes to think of herself as a good mother, a friend. Her son is named Tom. He looks like Tom. She loves her son but has never been able to like him.

Now, because it is dark, and summer, she sees only the reflection of her own face in the window of the train. It is a plain, calm face, lined around the mouth, with ice-blue eyes that she avoids looking into directly. Today is her anniversary. She and Tom were married eighteen years ago today, in the chapel of a country club with velveteen paintings hung on its walls, and then they went to Portugal. Tom wanted to see a bullfight, but Martha couldn't stomach the idea of watching as an animal was killed, so they compromised. In Portugal the fighters only tease the bull and stick him with darts but don't murder him.

They saw four fights in a week. There was much fuss made in the arena; the matadors and picadors marching around in fancy brocades, waving cloaks and weapons, and then the furious bull snorting and heaving and bowing toward the crowd. The crowd seemed subdued. Children cried and were slapped. By the end of each show, when the frustrated bull was led from the ring, he was decorated with his own blood, scarlet threads that swung from his slippery back. Tom smiled and went on stomping his feet. Leaving Portugal, in a cab on the way to the airport, Martha put a question to the driver, who spoke some English. "Why do the people of your country seem so sad?" she asked. Then she wished she hadn't, because he turned toward her and stopped watching the road. "They're not sad," he said. "They're just unhappy."

"I am not sad," she tells herself now, her face mouthing the words back at her from the window. "I am just unhappy." She thinks of her son. Tom Junior was born sad. Sadness is in his genes and he cannot shake it off; it's like a rotten name you have to live with. He is on his way home for the weekend, this minute, on the Throg's Neck Bridge in that broken-down car he played with all summer, both hands on the wheel, trembling. Traffic scares him. A lot of things frighten him. When he was very small she took him to the beach and put her bathing cap on and he screamed and ran away from her. Things like that. People pick on him. He phoned her last night from the state college in Oneonta where he has just started his first year. "Mom," he said. "I'm coming home a little while." He explained that he and his roommates, three other boys with whom he shared a suite in the dormitory, weren't getting along. Martha wondered, what does he mean they're not getting along? Are they all not getting along with each other, or are the three of them simply not getting along with him? "But they were matched with you on a computer," she found herself saying. "You had to fill out that form and they matched you up with those boys on a computer."

"It's a piece of trash," Tom said. He had pulled himself together. "Their computer's worthless. Everyone's switching roommates. Anyway I'm coming home. I'll go back Monday but I have to come home."

He hadn't mentioned the anniversary so she supposed he had forgotten about it. Previously they celebrated it together, just the two of them, just to have something to celebrate. They sat at the table in the dining room and ate a nice dinner and bad-mouthed Tom Senior and laughed. She liked to hear him poke fun at his father's tightfistedness. No money had been forthcoming to pay for his schooling. Or for his harmonicas. Tom Junior has six harmonicas, each tuned to a different key, and they cost fifteen dollars apiece and Tom Senior has not paid for a single one of them. That always gets a good laugh. But her son makes a habit, during these dinners, of trying to convince her to go out with other men. Some men have tried to get close to her over the years but she's turned them down. The idea of getting stuck with any one of them seemed ludicrous. Sometimes she has difficulty thinking of these men as men and of herself as a woman.

Turning from the window, Martha sees that the young woman reading the paper has left. The newspaper, rolled up on the seat, has been secured with a red rubber band. She wonders what kind of a woman would put the rubber band back on her newspaper when she has finished reading it, and she plucks at the rubber band with her fingernail until noticing that there is nobody else on the train with her. A heavy silence clings to the heat. The train has reached the last stop, her stop. She gathers her things, her tennis bag with the racket zipped to the outside, stuffed so tightly with her suit and blouse and high-heeled shoes that she couldn't quite close it, and her shopping bag with the Entenmann's cakes she bought at a bakery close to the office. She hunts for her purse. For a minute she thinks she has misplaced it but then she finds it in the shopping bag along with the cakes. She opens it and takes out her hairbrush. Her hair has recently been cut and shaped, so when she brushes it has a pleasant bounce. She brushes for a long time, keeping an eye on the sliding door to the compartment. Any minute, someone will come through and kick her out. She thinks if she still smoked cigarettes she would smoke one now. Then she stands up, and her thighs make that harsh sound as they are peeled from the vinyl seat.

The station platform is bare, bathed in a yellow light from the tall naked lamps that line the tracks. Because the train pulled in from the west, she is on the wrong side and has to climb the tinny steps to the footbridge that crosses over. But the air is damp and smoky and on the bridge it seems fresher; there is a breeze up there that smells of leaves.

Her car is parked in the long-term lot beyond the rows of cabs and the circular drive, in the dark. She is glad about the dark because suddenly she feels silly in the tennis dress. Her shoes make no sound as she crosses the pavement. At the car she stops, puts her things on the ground, bends over and rummages in the Entenmann's bag for her purse and keys. When she stands up there's a man with a hand on her shoulder. "Tom!" she says, because his face is in darkness and she thinks maybe her son has surprised her at the station, but it is not Tom because the man has a knife and has raised it to her throat.

"Lady," he says. "You got your car keys, lady?"

What's happening? she thinks, and throws the keys at his feet and ducks but he grabs her and makes her pick them up.

"I don't want your damn car keys," he says. "I want you to get in the car."

"You want me to unlock the car," she is saying. "You want me to get in the car," because she has heard that if you talk to a mugger like a human being then maybe he won't hurt you.

"Don't hurt me," she says.

"Very smart," he says, because she is working the keys in the lock, shoving each key in and yanking it out and fumbling.

"I don't have my car keys," she says. Her teeth are chattering. "I must have ... they must be," but he slashes her skirt with his knife.

"Lady," he says. "Do what I say."

She opens the door and for a second they stand there and look into the dimly lit interior of the car and at a pack of cough drops lying on the seat.

"Get in," he says.

She is thinking of the knife. She can think of nothing but the knife and the extraordinary noise it made when it cut into her skirt. Surely someone must have heard it, surely the cab drivers chatting in their smoky circle near the cabs heard it.

He has struck her arm, hard, with his fist, and she finds that she is seated in the car although she can't think how she got there.

"Move over," says the man.

He pushes her onto her back on the seat so her knee hits the steering wheel. The horn. The horn hasn't worked for ages but she pushes against it anyway with her knee, hoping to get a sound out of it.

"Don't kill me," she says. "Don't."

He has climbed into the car. He is leaning over her with the knife poised between their two bodies and he is grinning. She sees that he is terribly young.

"Now," he is saying.

"What?" she pleads. "Now what?" because she doesn't know what he is talking about. He slashes at the skirt again.

"Please," she says. "What? What do you want? Take the keys. The car. Take it."

"You know what I want."

"I don't. I don't know." Because she doesn't. The cakes? The tennis racket? Why won't he take it then and get away from her?

"Take it," she says. "Don't hurt me. Take what you want, I won't stop you."

But then there is the high wail of a police siren and the flashing red light as it pulls into the station drive.

After what seems like a long while she pulls herself up, gripping the steering wheel and pulling herself forward until her feet touch the pavement and she is sitting on the edge of the driver's seat looking out into the parking lot. It was not a police car after all but an ambulance that is parked at the station entrance with the light still turning and the back doors open. She sits there dully and watches the commotion. Only after someone has been carried out on a stretcher and the back doors have been slammed shut and the ambulance has driven off with its siren screaming does she realize what it was he must have wanted from her.

"Oh god," she says.

There is a bruise on her arm where he struck her and a spreading pain. Not much pain but she imagines it will get worse after a while as the shock wears off. She wonders if she is in shock. She doesn't know. She doesn't think so. She might call the police. There are phones in a row between the benches to the right of the station entrance. But she would have to walk through the parking lot to get to them. She thinks of screaming. If she screams, someone will come running and she can ask them to escort her to the telephones.

But what would she say to the police? There was this boy, and he pushed me into my car.

And she has nothing to show for it. Nothing but a slash here and there in the ridiculous pleated skirt of her tennis dress.

She pulls the Entenmann's bag and her tennis bag into the car. She puts them on the passenger seat and searches for her keys. They are dangling from the door. Then she starts for home, forgetting to turn on the lights until she is halfway across the parking lot and realizes that it's dark and she can't see anything.

Winter

One afternoon in early December, while Lydia was down in the basement printing T-shirts on a silk screen, snow fell. It was the first snow of the year and it didn't last very long; by the time she'd wiped the ink off her hands and climbed the steps to the kitchen it had stopped falling. When the wind blew over the hills, a faint white dusting of snow rippled underneath it like a bed sheet. This was in the outskirts of Charlottesville, Virginia, in a house that had belonged to a relative who died. It was a tall brick farmhouse with a rotting foundation; if you climbed to the second floor and looked out from the back you wouldn't see the city at all, just the layered blue hills and a thread of highway. Before this Lydia had been staying in Austin with a lover, and before that in Manhattan with a different lover, and before that in Philadelphia.

After a while a truck rolled up the drive and stopped in front of the house. A guy got out. Lydia thought at first he was looking for some wire to fix his muffler. The tail pipe was dragging. But then she recognized him as a man who played music in a couple of bars in town; he had blue eyes and a widow's peak and one night he'd come over to her table to admire her T-shirt. He wanted one for himself. He wanted a dragon, red on green, extra large. It felt good to be doing some business.

That evening it rained and the rain froze. John, who had planned to drive home to his wife, stayed with Lydia instead.

"Maybe you should call her," Lydia said.

They were lying on the mattress in her bedroom, flipping through sketch books. Ideas for T-shirts. John said not to worry, he didn't have to call his wife because he didn't care about her anymore because she didn't care about him. Last week she'd thrown a juice bottle at his head and missed and broke a window. All this after he bought her a washing machine. The kitchen smelled like sour oranges and if you walked in certain places your feet stuck to the linoleum.

"Wait," said Lydia. "Who stopped loving who first?"

"She never loved me in the first place," said John. "I just caught on."

There was a daughter, otherwise he'd move out for good. He wanted to go to New York City and get a band together and write songs and cut albums. For now he played bars and sold cocaine. He played a twelve-string with mother-of-pearl inlay, from a case lined with velvet scented like oil and wood. He was a huge man, fleshy and pale. Lydia liked the way the vial of cocaine looked, tiny in the palm of his hand.

After that it snowed five times in two and a half weeks and John was showing up every night. They'd walk out to the frozen water hole and skate around on their boot soles, or slide down the hill on a Hefty bag. Afterward they'd fill the tub with hot water and get in, one behind the other, and soap each other's backs. Asleep, John snored like a bear.

But on the morning of December 22 there was a thaw. The hills turned brown and yellow. John's tires got stuck in the mud, and finally Lydia had to take the wheel and rock the truck while he pushed from behind. Now she was standing alone in the kitchen, eating an apple for breakfast. An icicle fell past the window. "This is the first day of winter," she said, and then the phone rang. It was a woman.

"My name's Baby," said the woman. "In case he hasn't told you. I don't know what he's told you but it isn't true."

"Don't tell him I called," said Baby. "I just want you to stop loving him."

"Say something," said Baby. "I wanted to hear your voice."

"Maybe we should meet," said Lydia. She put the apple core on the windowsill and watched it. Maybe if she looked long enough it would turn brown.

"I don't know if I could stand to look at you," said Baby.

They met in the art museum. Baby had finally said yes, they could meet somewhere, as long as she could keep her eyes off Lydia and still have something to look at. She was wearing a sweat shirt with the name of a high school printed on it. She was taller than Lydia. She had large bones, a pale angular face, wide dark lips, and heavy eyelids. She looked like she wanted to shut her eyes.

"I was doing some laundry," Baby was saying, "with my new washer and dryer he bought me so I would be happy. He thinks when he goes to spend the night with you I can sit in the basement and watch the clothes go round and feel better. That's how I found your number, in the pocket of his jeans."

"I'm sorry," said Lydia.

They stopped walking, and stood before a large hanging screen titled "Mount Everest." If you looked closely enough you could make out the shape of the mountain like something scratched onto the paper with the tip of a needle. Closer up you saw the tiny scratched shapes of spruce trees. For a while they talked about John. They talked about his music. Lydia said she admired a man with aspirations. Baby said he'd been playing the same songs for years, that he'd never get anywhere except maybe jail or dead.

"You've got bird bones," said Baby. She had gone on to the next drawing. She still hadn't looked Lydia in the eye. "I bet he suffocates you," she said. "A man doesn't know his strength."

"We don't do it with him on top," said Lydia.

It was the wrong thing to say. Baby paled. She lifted her hands to her face. She had hair the color of copper that flashed about her shoulders. Lydia thought about touching her. She could put a hand on her shoulder, maybe push the hair from her face.

"Is that your real name?" she said finally, edging closer. "Baby?"

"Why don't you fall in love with someone else?" said Lydia.

She was crouched behind him in the tub, soaping his neck with a cloth. His neck was as big around as her thigh. When he lowered himself into the tub, water splashed over the sides.

"What?" said John.

"Fall in love with someone old and rich," said Lydia. "Then when they're dead and you're a millionaire, come back to me."

She was thinking of Baby's ring, a heavy band of cast silver with a jagged piece of turquoise set into it. John wore the same ring. Lydia hadn't noticed it before. Probably they were wedding rings. Baby's had a wad of masking tape wrapped around it, which meant she must have gotten thinner since the wedding day.

Now the soap was lost. They started feeling around, touching one another under the clouded water. If they wanted to get really clean they'd have to empty the tub and start over again. Lydia sniffed at the back of his neck and under his arms where the hair was still thick with lather. She liked how he smelled. He smelled like a clean animal.

"I've got it," she said.

"Okay," said John. "Don't let go."

Later that night he made a phone call and told Lydia he was driving up to Culpepper to visit Rick and Sue, friends of his. He said she could come if she wanted, so she made coffee and poured it into a thermos and climbed into the truck with him. The truck didn't have any heat but it was a warm night, the kind of night in which crickets would sing if it were summer.

"We're decorating," said Sue when she met them at the door. She was holding one end of a string of Christmas bulbs. Rick, who had the other end, was trying to push his way between the couch and the wall so he could plug it in.

"Next year I said to Rick we'll have to go on a diet so we have room for a tree," said Sue. She laughed. Both of them were fat. You couldn't guess their ages. On the mantelpiece was a photo of Sue when she wasn't fat and in the photo she looked about sixteen.

Suddenly the lights in Sue's hand blinked on, and she laughed. John played a couple of songs on his guitar, and after each one Sue laughed again, and clapped. Rick made some lines on a mirror and passed it around, and Lydia found herself telling Sue she liked her dress. It was a sleeveless dress with strawberries on it, the kind of dress you'd wear if you were fat and happy. The night went on; every so often the lights blinked. Lydia thought she could have known these people for years, she could be sitting here forever in this cozy room. To get to the bathroom you had to walk through a narrow hallway to the bedroom, where the bed was unmade. There was a dent in the middle of the mattress, which meant they rolled together as they slept, and on the sheets were roses, tiny hard clusters of them.

Back in the living room Rick handed her a chocolate cookie the size of a pancake and said, "Here, Baby." At first Lydia thought he was being affectionate but then she realized he was calling her by Baby's name, and that he and Sue thought she was Baby. There hadn't been any introductions.

When they left it was nearly dawn. Sue filled the thermos with fresh coffee and said they should come back again, maybe eat dinner with the television on. At the doorway Rick gave John a package, and John gave Rick twelve hundred dollars.

By December 31 there had been two weeks of rain and sun and the earth was muddy. The air was fresh. Buds appeared on the trees. People said it was a freak year, winter come and gone already, spring on the way. Lydia drove into town and set her table up, on a sidewalk in front of some shops. Sunlight bounced off the shop windows, warming her back. In five hours she sold seven dragon T-shirts, four Mad Hatters, eight unicorns, and five Medusas. For summer, she was thinking, she'd do a winged horse, yellow on white. People would buy it, she was thinking, for the same reason they bought the dragons and the unicorns: they were unhappy with their lives. Someone tapped her on the arm. It was Baby, her hair flashing like a penny.

"You look good," said Lydia. "But thin."

Baby seemed puzzled. "I like those shirts," she said. "I was wondering if you have one small enough for a kid five and a half years old."

"I can give you the extra small," said Lydia, "and you can wash it hot and stick it in the dryer."

She felt bad, having mentioned the washer and dryer. It was like saying John's name. But Baby didn't seem to mind. She took an orange shirt with a red dragon on it.

"How much?" she said, digging around in the pockets of her jeans. You could see her hip bones pushing through the cloth.

"Take it," said Lydia. "I wouldn't sell you a shirt."

"Is there something wrong with it?" said Baby, pulling at the seams with her fingernails.

Then she looked at Lydia hard and refolded the shirt and put it back on the table on top of the others and walked away. A few yards off she stopped.

"I didn't know you had those crooked teeth," she said. "I don't see how he loves you."

When she had gone Lydia loaded the shirts and the folding table and the money box into the back seat of her car, and then she slid into the front seat and lowered the visor and looked at her face in the mirror. It was true about the crooked teeth. They'd grown in like that. She liked them. She liked her imperfections. They made her feel human.

At home John was standing in the middle of her bedroom, unpacking a suitcase, hanging his shirts in the closet next to Lydia's shirts.

"You moving in finally?" she asked.

"Looks like it," he said.

For New Year's Eve there was a bottle of sparkling wine from the supermarket. John was happy with himself for remembering it. They heated some up in a pot, with orange slices and pieces of apple and banana. In the wine, the fruit turned purple. John played songs. His face changed when he sang. In the candlelight the burnished face of the guitar had the texture of silk. Lydia got restless; she found a broom and a dustpan and swept the house, the kitchen first, the hallway, the steps. She swept in the dark. She was thinking how a year ago on New Year's she and Bruce bought five six-packs at a 7-Eleven in Austin, and how a year before that she had dinner with Michael in a Trader Vic's on Staten Island. She thought how the New Year always made you think back, never ahead. For a minute she was mixed up and saw Bruce on Staten Island, Michael in Texas, John somewhere else.

"I have to clear my head," she said, and went out to the porch with a blanket, thinking that when she came back in they could turn the TV on and watch the ball dropping over Times Square, then all the old couples dancing.

"You tell him the landlord's here, and it's the first of the month, and I can't pay the rent even for last month let alone this month, and Virginia's got chicken pox, and he better tell me what it is I'm supposed to do," said Baby.

"He's in the shower," Lydia said. He was singing in the shower. She pulled the telephone receiver away from her ear; Baby was screaming into it: "So I'm supposed to tell my landlord wait till my husband gets out of the shower at Lydia's house and then maybe I can pay the rent?"

There was a pause, Baby sniffing at the other end.

"You could give your landlord the washing machine," said Lydia.

"What?" said Baby.

"And then the dryer for next month," said Lydia.

In the silence that followed she heard the shower stop. She could have called John to the phone.

"Or I could write you a check," she said.

Baby lived in a neighborhood on the opposite edge of town; to get there you had to take a road down into Charlottesville and then another road up a hill past the university. The house sat on top of a sloping yard reinforced with railroad ties, and since there didn't seem to be a driveway Lydia parked on the street and climbed up. The house was pumpkin-colored, with an ornate porch and irregular glass in the windows. Baby lived in one half of the bottom floor. There were beer cans stacked in her window. She came to the door in a bathrobe, shaking a thermometer.

"Virginia's got fever," she said. "Look at that snow."

Either the snow had just started or Lydia hadn't noticed it on the drive over; it fell thickly and steadily past. Baby didn't ask her to come inside. She stood in the doorway. She said the landlord had gone home for his lunch and would come back later for the check, which better have Lydia's social security number and driver's license number and telephone number printed on the back of it. Then she took the check and turned it over a couple of times, to make sure it wasn't a fake.

"If I told John you were doing this I wouldn't go home if I was you," said Baby.

She was staring past Lydia at some roofs that were turning white, then she lifted a hand to her chest and pressed the flat part of her wrist against the hollow of her chest and held it there. Lydia understood this to be a gesture that Baby made often, a habit, her hand on her heart, her heart beating under it, for solace. She kept her own hands flat at her sides. There was nothing to do; she wished she hadn't come. She turned away into the weather, where the fat neat flakes dropped silently under their own weight. How perfect they were in their last moment, in that brief cold moment before they hit the earth.

How to Live Alone

Steven's ghost is breathing on her neck. His breath is salty and warm. It seems to come from far off. She knows it's Steven; on the beach first thing that morning he began reading her book from over her shoulder and turning the pages just as Steven used to, impatiently flipping them as she was finishing the last line. There was that same tremor of agitation, his fingers drumming on the jacket of the book. It was uncanny how he'd always known exactly when to turn the pages, never a second too early or late. But it isn't so uncanny anymore. Nancy sits quietly in her beach chair till dusk, reading along with him, even after all the other bathers have packed their towels and gone home and there are shadows. The tide quits moving inches from her feet. The sand stays warm.

There have been other things. Hints. The first, last night just after she'd arrived, had been enough to let her know someone was there. She had left Lloyd Harbor later than she'd planned, having fallen asleep over dinner and then wakened embarrassed to find herself drooling, spit on her chin. She wrapped her plate in foil and set it in the refrigerator on top of last night's dinner, then put her slippers on and walked out to the car, which was already packed. She had to unload the trunk and find shoes. Sneakers. You can't drive in slippers—suppose you get a flat or run out of gas on the highway? She began to think about going to bed and waiting for morning. She could leave at five and beat the traffic. Instead she drove to the 7-Eleven for coffee and drank it standing in the parking lot, watching some teenagers smoke cigarettes. When the coffee was gone she walked back into the 7-Eleven and bought a pack of Nows and lit one. She lit a second in the car and smoked through Lake Ronkonkoma, then tossed the pack under her seat where she couldn't reach it. The drive was no fun—there was darkness and smog and finally turning onto West Hampton Beach she had to strain to see the railings of the bridge. In the rear-view mirror she saw her own pale face with the fog around it. It looked drained and gray, and it made her think of ghosts.

The apartment, which they'd bought six years ago for summer weekends, was on the bay side of Dune Road. Steven had wanted the bay side so he could take his sailfish out in the evenings while Nancy sat on the deck and watched. Time after time he'd strained against the bright triangle of sail toward the opposite shore, his hair glistening silver. He'd have a wet suit on. Coming back he'd be ruddy with cold and she'd unzip him. She went out to the deck the minute she arrived, and stood leaning with her hands flat against the railing in the fog that smelled salty and woody from the reeds. There were rabbits there with their eyes lit up. She could hear the tall dry stalks of the reeds breathing against one another, and the slow lapping of the water. In the stillness she felt the sounds advancing upon her.

Later, in her robe in the tiny kitchen, she thought she'd pour herself a glass of wine. It was jug wine. Why buy a good wine when there was only one of you? She wanted half a glass. She couldn't remember the glasses ever being so large. But she was prevented from turning the bottle upright. The wine kept gushing out, a ribbon of pink that bubbled when it struck the glass. It was as if a hand had been lowered onto the neck of the bottle and was holding it down until finally the glass was filled and the bottle sprang back as if the hand had been pulled away from it.

Later she recalled Steven's insistence that she take more wine than she wanted on the nights he intended to make love to her.

And a door had opened by itself. Had it been an ordinary door she would have thought nothing of it; there were plenty of breezes near the water and doors were always being blown open. But this was a sliding door made of glass. It led from the bedroom onto a tiny slatted porch overlooking the parking lot. It had been closed. Then it was open. She was climbing into bed when she noticed it, the curtains billowing. So she stepped out for a minute in her nightgown to look around.

You couldn't see the ocean from there but you could hear it. There was nothing else. Only she found herself peering at the flower boxes, which were still papery with dead geraniums from a year ago. They'd been infested. Steven had cared for them. At night in his underwear he'd pinched the gluey white eggs from the joints of the stems, shining a pocket flashlight up under the leaves while he crouched below them.

Nancy is fifty-one years old. She has always been thin but now she is thinner. She has brought with her to the apartment on West Hampton Beach six books including four cheap novels, a guide to the shorebirds that Steven had taken along every summer and never opened, and a dictionary with a broken spine. In the months since Steven's death she has discovered in herself a certain poverty of words; she does not have the words to make her truest feelings understandable even to herself. It seems wasteful to her, that a woman should spend hours picking through her emotions in search of the one she can name. Her plan for the summer consists simply of circling in the dictionary those words whose definitions seem to apply to herself. Later, in the fall, she'll type them up, weed some out, reread the list each day and pare it like a fruit until she has to stop, until there remains only a hardened core of words that she might swallow and expel. So far she's circled just two. "Age" is the first, and that doesn't help. When you're fifty-one you know how old you are. Just the same, a spot on her cheek below the left eye has recently started to twitch. Of course. You get old. If it takes the death of your husband to bring it on, who's to say you weren't lucky having lasted that long? They'd found a bunch of roses in his car. They'd handed them to her along with the news. Imagine opening the door to some cop breathing roses, tears in his eyes.

The second word, "afflux," the act of traveling toward a point, she'd circled without really knowing why. She used a red pen; the circle gave the word a misspelled look. If she was traveling toward a point, would she know when she was there? Maybe not. The vanishing point. She'd set the roses in a soup can she'd emptied for supper. She forgot to put water in.

After the funeral she drove six hours to Stamford, Connecticut, where Steven's younger sister lived in a high-rise. Jolene was fat and had swollen arteries and couldn't make it to Long Island by herself. Years ago she'd switched her name from Jody, hoping the change would make her less fat. Still, people called her Jody by mistake. She blamed them for her inability to shed weight. Nancy and Steven had called her Jolene; for this they were mammothly loved. Jolene, finding Nancy at the door, cried out and swaddled her in pounds of milky flesh. She had been weeping, more than usual. The front of her blouse was transparent with tears. She grabbed hold of Nancy's suitcase. Nancy wondered if she'd brought enough to last.

"Tell me how it happened," wept Jolene. "They told me he was bringing you flowers."

"Yes," Nancy said. "But who says the flowers were meant for me?"

Jolene dried her eyes and stared hard.

"He wasn't in the habit of bringing me flowers," Nancy went on. "When there wasn't an occasion."

"Do I hear what you're saying?" yelled Jolene. She had taken Nancy's hand in hers. For a fat woman Jolene had lovely hands, sharp and delicate.

"It's just a thought," Nancy said. "He was driving through Great Neck when he died. As far as I know there was absolutely no reason on earth Steven would be in Great Neck."

"There must be some way to find out!" said Jolene. "You have a right to know!" Her hard little blue eyes blinked.

"I don't care to," said Nancy.

That night there was a tremendous thump and Nancy got up to check on things. She was sleeping in Jolene's room, under the white and sky-blue comforter that gave her bed the plump appearance of a cloud. Jolene had insisted on spending the night in the living room. It wasn't the type of couch that folded out into a bed and it was far too narrow for Jolene. She had tipped too far in the wrong direction and rolled off. There she lay on the floor, her body quivering beneath the gauze of a nightgown. She had not woken up. She was dreaming. She was dreaming of love, her perfect hands searching the air above her. Nancy stood in the doorway a minute and looked at her and wondered what to do. Wake her up? Let her sleep? Maybe this was the kind of thing you should expect in a woman who lived by herself, that she wake up each day in a heap on the floor not knowing how she got there, when she fell, when the crash occurred. Jolene was moaning. Her mouth was wide open and you could see the moonlight inside of it.

The visit was otherwise uneventful. Jolene showed Nancy photographs of her and Steven growing up. She cried, Nancy comforted. Jolene still wore her high school ring, gold plate with a dull blue stone.

Nancy left Stamford two days early and drove back through Manhattan on a Friday. It was early May, the sun on the sidewalks glaring like snow. She meant to buy herself some tinted glasses, the kind whose lenses darkened when you stepped outside. Instead she chose a pair in an aviator style whose lenses didn't change but gave the world, inside and out, a smoky look. The sidewalks glistened not like snow but like water, like a place where water has been once and slipped back. Then in Saks she moved among the dresses restfully, touching the fabrics and letting them brush against her. She craved summer. The dresses were smooth and cool and airy. At last she bought a blouse, silk, in a dusky salmon color.

At home in Lloyd Harbor, later that evening with her sunglasses off, Nancy found that her blouse wasn't salmon at all but hot pink. She started to cry. She hadn't cried a bit since Steven's death; instead her eyes stayed dry and numb. She cried for a long time and walked aimlessly through the huge house. She turned the television on and watched the end of the sports news, then listened to the weather announcer's jokes. Sobbing seemed shocking and dangerous, as if she'd swallowed some poor animal that was trying to get out. But her eyes were soothed. At the end she blew her nose into the blouse and balled it up and stuffed it in the garbage and dumped some coffee grounds on top of it. Then she walked three blocks to Walter Sneider's house. He was the family doctor, a divorcé of fifteen years, balding, with large ears you could trace the veins in. For ages Nancy had chosen his carpets and drapes and upholsteries, and had supervised their installation, always keeping in mind what Greta, his absent wife, would have chosen herself. Florals mostly, prolific and unmatched like some dense fruity jungle, sachets in the closets, strawberry soaps. Walter himself was a sudden cool comfort, like waking between new sheets. He made her a rum punch, he smelled of lime, he was solicitous as always and gave her the softest chair to sit in and then ran a bath without her knowing, in the black-tiled bathroom.

Then he toweled her dry and stood her on the scale and weighed her.

"You've lost weight," he scolded. "Look at these ribs. You need a rest, Nancy. You're in shock. You need some time alone."

Three nights later he brought it up again. They had gone to a movie and were sitting in his car. The parking lot was jammed with cars and people pushing to get past. The movie was *Breaker Morant,* and Nancy couldn't speak. She saw the two men tied to their chairs on a high rocky plain in South Africa, waiting to be shot, and then the credits floating past, and Walter's smooth pink brow as he turned to her and led her from the theater. It was hot in Walter's car but his words stirred her.

"You still have that place out east," he said. "In the Hamptons. Go there and I'll join you in a week or two. Don't worry if you find you want to sleep in the middle of the day. Drink plenty of cold water. Collect shells."

His voice and touch were soothing and familiar. Waking with him close to her each morning, staring at his wide and freckled body, Nancy longed for West Hampton Beach.

Steven has no interest in the dictionary game. Nancy feels him wander off toward the water. She strains, shades her eyes, and sees a wave part and come together where his ankles would have been. He leaves neither shadow nor footprint; she senses his presence the way a blind person senses a door, by some shift in the intensity of light and air. When he comes near, the hairs on Nancy's arm stand up and hold the sunlight close to her.

She circles "Ally." "Alongside." The word "Alone," uncircled, between them on the page, looks blank and mute and forceful. This morning at breakfast (a hard roll with butter and marmalade, a pot of coffee small enough to brew a single cup, a dish of raspberries in milk), Nancy felt his hunger yawning near her, as bottomless and needy as a black hole in space. She felt helpless in the face of it. She wanted to feed him. She broke the roll in two and spread the jam on thick and placed it on the table in front of him. Then she turned toward the bay and watched a man rowing out in a clam boat, hoping that when she turned back to look for it the roll would have vanished. But it was there. She broke it into pieces and tossed them into the reeds where the birds would eat them.

The barn swallows, which nested every year beneath the high cedar deck, kept darting in and out in their swift, silent way. Their wings flashed blues and purples. To Nancy their perpetual swooping had the exact quality of those stabs of pain you read about in books, a sudden plunging sadness like an arrow in the heart. Grief, she thought, would pierce the air like this, like birds feeding over the saw grass, hovering and diving, vanishing and reappearing.

But Nancy wasn't feeling any grief. She felt remote and cool sitting there, her breakfast untouched, a radio playing behind her. The swallows were merely a lesson in sadness, one of those trade books, *Coping with Widowhood,* you read reviews about dry-eyed. It was all right; here was Steven in the deck chair next to hers, keeping her coffee warm. That had been one of his habits, placing a hand palm down on her coffee cup to keep it hot for her.

Now Nancy puts the dictionary down and joins him at the water. The tide is out, the surface of the ocean calm and bright. Gulls chatter on the wet sand and in the air above. Nancy is wearing a straw beach hat, her black swimsuit, and her wading pants, a pair of army fatigues cut off at the knees. Steven has a pair as well. The two of them walk west, past the crazy beach houses and rows of umbrellas, under the high noon sun in silence. They have always walked this way, Nancy on the outside stopping every now and then for shells, Steven on the inside. He likes the chill of the water, the sting. There was always this companionable silence. On the jetty though, climbing the wet black ribbon of rock, Nancy worries. What if he slips, falls, hurts himself? How would she know or help? Who's to say a man can't die a second time, leaving his ghost on the rocks like an echo?

At home, dizzy and smarting from the sun, Nancy fumbles with the key. The telephone is ringing, insistently, as if it's been at it all day. Walter, thinks Nancy. Probably he's ready to come out. What can she tell him? *Don't come. Steven will be hurt.*

It isn't Walter but his wife, Greta Sneider, who for fifteen years has run a dancing school for little girls in Great Neck, in a tired old house as leafy and gracious as a stranded yacht. Nancy imagines rows of leotarded girls in tap shoes, Greta keeping time with a gardenia. She and Walter communicate only on birthdays; Greta sends him bolts of cloth, vanilla beans, tiny corked bottles of orange blossom water, things he doesn't know what to do with.

"Nancy," she says. "Are you holding up?"

"Thank you, yes," says Nancy. "How did you know I was here?"

"I knew. I don't know."

"You must have tried the house."

"No. I would have tried there next. How's your back?"

"My back?" says Nancy.

"I thought it was troubling you."

"No," says Nancy. Although she had bruised her back a little several months ago, playing squash with Steven. "But thank you."

"Of course. Don't ask me how I'm doing. I'm up to my neck in tutus. It's absolutely loony. But call me if you need me," says Greta. "If you need someone to talk to."

"Thank you," says Nancy, and she hangs up, feeling foolish. When at a loss for words she always says thank you, over and over. This makes her feel empty-handed, like someone waiting for a gift that doesn't come.

Absently, Nancy lifts the spice rack from the wall near the telephone and runs her hand along the bottom of the shelf. It had been Steven's idea to hide it there, the Glad Bag of marijuana he'd shocked her with last summer. He said he wanted to know what the fuss was about. So they'd smoked some. But it wasn't much, after all. It merely caused her to examine the most ordinary things with great care and attention to detail, the way you'd study an expensive piece of clothing you were thinking of buying. So the flaws in her life became suddenly clearer and manageable; she remembers plucking her eyebrows, writing an overdue letter, calling a friend who had borrowed a favorite book and not returned it. When she had tired of all this, she slept, dreamlessly.

"Christ," Nancy says. It's impossible to get the thing rolled. She knows you're supposed to clean the marijuana before rolling it but she doesn't know which part to get rid of. So everything keeps slipping from between her fingers or sticking out at odd angles, tearing the flimsy rectangle of paper.

"I really don't see why *you* can't roll this thing," Nancy says to the ghost. "You always wanted to do it."

"Please," she says, after a silence.

"At least," she says, "show me how."

She thinks if a ghost talked it would be in a whisper, a sound as deep and cryptic as a heartbeat. She listens very hard. There is nothing to hear, but all at once she finds she's picked up the cigarette and rolled it. It is there in her hand, a perfect tapered cylinder.

She lights it and smokes, with her head thrown back and her feet on the table, thinking vaguely of Greta and Steven. Were they lovers? But what really seems to matter is the smoke itself, keeping it inside, trapping the coughing spells. Steven had put it that way. "You have to trap those coughs before they can escape," he'd say, "like farting in company."

Nothing happens, except that she gets up from the couch and goes into the bathroom, where she removes her wading pants, her swimsuit, even her watch. For a while she stands in front of the mirror, not looking at herself. She turns the fan on so the room can breathe. From the medicine cabinet she pulls the wide blue bottle of Nivea cream. She squeezes it, and two worms of white lotion drop from it onto her legs. Then her belly and arms, her neck, feet, breasts, all of her. She watches as the cream disappears beneath her hands, into her skin, which has a reptilian look from the salt and sun. She feels graceful and self-absorbed and private, the way she used to feel when, preparing to go out, she'd barred Steven from the bathroom and readied herself in the close, steamy place.

In the living room again, wrapped in nothing but a towel, Nancy notices the painting hanging on the wall above the couch. It is one of her own, a seascape she did years ago in a night class at C. W. Post. The sun on the rocks looks like yellow paint someone spilled on them. And the painting is hanging at an angle, something Steven never would allow. He can't stand the sight of a crooked painting, he would have straightened it—even in museums he had embarrassed her by reaching out and tapping on the corners of the frames.

Then, looking at the beige carpet and the ivory couch and the cream walls and the dusky view of the bay through the glass, Nancy knows how empty the room has become, how quiet and still and pale, like a tide pool the water has seeped out of.

She calls Walter. He sounds breathless and pleased.

"I'm on my way," he says. "You caught me checking the oil. I'm a grease ball."

"Don't come," Nancy says.

"Excuse me?" says Walter.

"Don't come," she repeats. "I need more time. I'm sorry."

After a minute Walter says, "I'll come on Saturday instead. I've got these lobsters. Should I cook them or freeze them till then?"

"Eat them," Nancy says.

It is late August, the deck in orange sunlight. Swans feed in the water at the lip of the bay where the reeds thin out. Beyond them that clam boat floats, shallow and rocking, that man wading round it with his rake and sack. Nancy has begun to feel edgy. She reminds herself periodically of the money she'd collect were she to put this place up for rent, or better still, sell the house in Lloyd Harbor. She's heard stories of widows who sell their estates and move into carriage houses on the edges of horse farms. She thinks of doing something like that, but not quite like that. She thinks of Manhattan, of the bustle and excitement, how she ought to find herself a home in the middle of things. And then a job in a shop. She could buy her own shop or start a business; she has that knack for interior design. Truthfully, she has been musing about this for days; she sees herself strolling through the entranceways of other people's houses bearing armloads of paint samples and fabrics, floorings, wallpapers, and carpets. She would alter people's lives. They'd call her, she'd come. For the moment, though, it's dinner time. Nancy snips the thorns from the leaves of an artichoke. She'll eat it with butter and garlic and allow herself the pleasure of a book while she eats. One of the mysteries.

In October Nancy rents a room in a luxury hotel in Manhattan. On her first evening she takes a ride in one of those horse-drawn carriages; leaves are falling in the park, and the lights are blinking on in the buildings surrounding it. There's a man with a bouquet of pinwheels, and a group of young women carrying musical instruments, and another woman holding an umbrella, although it isn't raining. Later, in her room, Nancy drinks a small amount of brandy and falls asleep feeling warm and impatient but a little lonely.

Next morning, drinking coffee in the high-ceilinged dining room, she notices a man, a young man wearing a brown suit, alone at a table. He's got his eyes shut tight and his hands clasped under his chin. Is he praying? All around him the waiters are hurrying and people are chattering. The sight of him fills her with pity and hope, as if she's come upon a person waltzing alone in a ballroom. There's a plate with a roll and a pot of jam, and the neat white tablecloth, and the pot of coffee. Nancy studies his lips as they move. She can't make herself stop staring. She presses forward in her chair and strains to hear his thanks being lifted away from him.

Trees at Night

"But I wouldn't call them rapes," Mandy is saying. "I mean he didn't really do it. Or maybe they just managed to fight him off before he got to it. They said he hid behind a tree. He was emaciated! A shrimp! But a lot of them start out that way, low key, and then they become more..."

"Aggressive," David says.

"Violent." Mandy's face screws up when she says this, and David sees that she really is frightened. A moment comes and goes, familiarly, when he sees himself reaching out to touch her, but as usual the inclination is not specific enough to be acted upon; he cannot see just what his hand might do when it reaches her, what part of her he might touch, and how, and for how long. He would like to touch her cheekbones. In fact he would like to touch her entire face the way a blind person would, with the tips of his fingers, but because they aren't lovers there seems no way of going about it. She really is striking, in an emotional sort of way, so that what she feels is mirrored in her face as if by an artist, and David imagines that by touching her he might better understand her. He once told her this.

"What's there to understand?" she asked. "I'm all here, I'm not deep, I'm not hiding anything. I don't think I have any secrets. I'm not that kind of person, am I? It's all dramatics, really." She made a face at him, sticking her tongue out.

At ten-thirty Mandy stands up to rinse her wine glass in the sink, carelessly as usual, so the glass strikes the porcelain with a ringing sound.

"Oh, did I break it? No." She holds it up and twirls it so he can see. David is relieved; the glass is one of four he bought a short time ago at Woolworth's, a cheap set, with seams in their stems like the seams in hosiery, but he likes them—they're not fancy, they suit him. Mandy dries hers on the curtain and wipes her hands on her blue jeans.

"You should get a dish towel."

"Bachelors don't buy dish towels."

"I once slept with a man who didn't have toilet paper. I had to use a wash cloth and rinse it out." Mandy laughs and makes a joke about how David is to watch her through the window to be sure she gets home safely. She lives next door. She never follows the sidewalk but cuts across the lawn, through the tall, ill-cut grass, high-stepping in her awkward sandals. "Why do women wear sandals like that?" says David to the window pane.

Several minutes later, Mandy's boyfriend Eric bicycles up the driveway, jumps off the seat, unclips his pants cuff, and follows Mandy inside with the light still clipped to his arm, the white beam dancing alongside of him.

Soon David goes out for his dog walk, around the reservoir barefoot. It's his private joke, that he walks an invisible dog on these chilly excursions, a dog that follows him the way dogs always do, by walking ahead of him. In springtime, the high school kids aren't out there screwing yet, and the night has a presence all its own that floats above the ripples in the water, without seeming to touch it. David enjoys the brief, quiet circle he makes on the dirt path, never stopping to sit. He is somewhat overweight, and he can see himself sitting on the slatted bench, a fat man staring into black water.

Mandy and her boyfriend aren't having an easy time. They're not fighting, simply moving past one another. "Near misses" is the term Mandy favors, with a slight, quick raising of her eyebrows. Sometimes she experiments with paying Eric some attention, beginning by asking some inappropriate question about a graphic he's been working on, on a subject requiring such technical expertise that she'll need to ask him to rephrase his answer even though they both know she's not really interested.

"The same thing happens the other way around," she says to David.

"But why *should* you be interested in each other's jobs?" he says. "Day in and day out, it's irrelevant. That seems to me to be something you would have worked out by now."

"It's not the jobs," Mandy says. "I don't even care if he cares about his job, much less about mine. What bothers me is I don't know if I care about him anymore. Or if he cares about me."

"But do you *care* if he cares about you," David jokes. Mandy shrugs, not getting it. "It seems to me that you can go through stages like this and then grow out of them and start caring about one another in different ways," he continues.

"This isn't a stage, David. It's not as if we had a crush on each other and now we have to get to know each other better."

"Maybe you just don't like each other anymore, then."

"Thanks."

"You talk to me like I don't have any idea what you're going through, and then you get pissed off when I don't make it better," says David.

"You *don't* have any idea what I'm going through, but you *do* make it better."

"I don't see why it's so important for two people to stay together," says David gloomily.

"I know. Sometimes I think I should marry him, so he can divorce me. I keep thinking of this one Thanksgiving we had together, when things were really good between us. Not a long time ago. I made a turkey, and all the things that go with it. Stuffing, cranberries, potatoes..."

David nods. Mandy stops talking long enough to pour herself more wine. Her third glass, and still she focuses deliberately, gripping it, so her fingers clenched around the stem make David think a wine glass must be like an egg—no matter how hard you hold onto it, it won't break.

"I spent all day cooking, or just hanging out in the kitchen, because it was so cozy in there. The windows steamed up, and it was snowing out. Eric was watching football. I didn't even mind he was watching football, because it seemed so homey, him lying on his back on the bed while I cooked, just down the hallway. Have you ever stewed cranberries? They pop! When they heat up! It was such a great day. We made love a little, and then we sat down to eat, and it was over in fifteen minutes. We just ate it like any other dinner, because we couldn't work up the mood, the whole Thanksgiving thing, after having eaten together every night for months in front of the news. I was so disappointed. I kept stuffing myself just so we could keep sitting there pretending."

David says he solved the problem of Thanksgiving by ignoring it and cooking a hamburger unless he was seeing Julie at the time and they went out. They once went to a Chinese place that served American-style Thanksgiving food with fortune cookies at the end. Julie wouldn't let him read her fortune, which at the time seemed important to him and triggered an "off" period that they later laughed about whenever they were "on."

"What was it?" asks Mandy.

"She never told me."

Mandy purses her lips and sips a little wine. Later, after Mandy has gone home, David phones Julie.

"What was that fortune?" he asks.

"None of your business."

"Come on."

"Something about how beautiful I was." Julie is not beautiful. "I was embarrassed to show it to you."

"Should I come up for the night?"

"Not really."

"Someone's there?"

"More or less."

The ambiguity is Julie's style, and he admires the way she makes it sound absolute.

"In a couple of days, maybe," she says. "What's new in your life?"

"Nothing. I'm still trying to figure out if I should try and make it with Mandy or not."

That night there's another attack, and again the woman, a student jogging, breaks free and sprints back to her dorm. She does not scream. The policeman, who comes to talk with David on the following morning, identifies the tree behind which the man hid as one in David's front yard, one whose leaves can be seen from David's gabled bedroom window.

"She said he was narrow," the policeman snorts. David nods, looking at the sycamore, which is young, upright, but comparatively small. He is glad that the girl didn't scream, because he heard nothing. How awful it would be if she screamed and no one came. However, it is not the girl he thinks of after the policeman drives off but the attacker himself, who stood waiting on David's lawn as David lay inside reading, the glow of his bedside lamp visible among the branches of the tree. David can't think of a lonelier thing.

But he can't say that to Mandy. He tells her he was reading the book she loaned him, Katherine Mansfield's letters. Love letters to John Middleton Murray. Pages and pages of "Darlings" and "Sweethearts," the same frank, hungry language over and over.

"How can one person have written so many letters? I feel like a Peeping Tom, reading them. I think I'm falling in love with her."

"And she wanted him to burn them," says Mandy. "Think of it. You have a love affair now, no one will ever know, you do it on the *telephone*. No one writes letters. Think of listening in on her phone calls!"

"You liked reading them as much as I do."

"I felt like a Peeping Tom too," she admits.

"Peeping Mandy."

"Yeah. Only from inside. It's my new hobby. Don't you just want to look and see if he's out there?"

"Who?"

"Behind that tree again."

"Oh." He comes up from behind her and parts the curtains. She's been standing there all along, twirling her wine glass, wanting to look out the window. He didn't know. They stare out across the yard, above the spiky crowns of some shrubs, to the plane trees with their flaking, layered, silvery bark, the trunks like satin where the bark is stripped. A week has passed since the assault. Women, if they walk alone, follow the center of the road as if walking a tightrope. David has noticed that the ones who walk alone have about them an exaggerated energetic bravery, their shoulder bags swinging freely from their elbows, flat leather boots slap-slapping the pavement.

"I like them," Mandy says. "I admire them. Only I couldn't do it, I'm too scared. Eric says it shows, that I'm scared, and that that's how they choose their victims. Evidently he's saying if I get it, I asked for it."

"No, he isn't. He's protecting you."

"He says if I can't sleep, I might try not drinking so much wine over here every night. Wine keeps me up. I fall asleep, and then I wake up a few hours later dehydrated. I think he resents you."

"I didn't know you weren't sleeping," says David, concerned. But then the telephone rings. It's Julie, wanting to come down.

"Bring egg rolls," David says into the receiver. He grins at Mandy, who puffs out her cheeks. Julie lives near a Chinese takeout, where the cashier calls her Dollie.

"Bye," says Julie.

"Bye, Dollie," says David.

"Who's Dollie?" asks Mandy, looking amused.

"Julie. She's coming over. How can Eric resent me?"

"Not you, I guess. He resents me for needing to come here. I guess I better go."

"I'll walk you home."

"It's not necessary."

"Just scream, then."

"Wonderful. I should practice walking to the corner and back. Naked. Carrying a tomahawk. A boa constrictor."

"I once picked up a hitchhiker," says David. "A girl. She gets in the car and takes an apple from her bag and starts peeling it, with this giant knife. The whole ride she's peeling it, continuously, so the skin doesn't tear, and then she cuts it into eighths, real methodically, and picks out the seeds with the tip of the blade. I was scared out of my wits."

"You were scared!" Mandy puts on her sandals, and then she has to take them off again to put her socks on first. She wears lavender socks, turned down at the ankles, and pants to mid-calf, a girl's costume, David always thinks, except her legs are strong, unshaven, the hair a fine, dark shadow. At once he is jealous, not of Eric himself but of the fact of Eric coming home through that kitchen door, where the vestibule is piled messily with socks and shoes, a tangle of male and female—sneakers, sandals, boots, slippers, the socks grass-stained, their toes threadbare. It's not true what he told her, about the hitchhiker and the apple. Or maybe it happened, but to somebody else, somebody who passed it on. The thing is, when he told the story, he believed he was telling the truth, for in the few seconds that it took to tell, he could feel it happening. He felt the girl's fear and his own emotion bouncing off it, like opposing poles of a single magnet, fear and longing, longing and fear.

"What I mean is," says Mandy, squinting into his gaze, "do you think I want to love Eric but I don't, or I don't want to love him but I do?"

"I think you want to love him and you do love him. You come over here because you like all the free booze you get out of me."

"You're right," Mandy laughs, and is gone, the door swinging open behind her. David cleans the kitchen and changes his clothes, into fresh black jeans and a black knit shirt with the full moon silk-screened on it. His loony shirt. When Julie arrives, the door is still open. For a second she stands on the step as if the door is a mystery, something to be wary of, but she's invulnerable. Stepping inside she drops the shopping bag in David's lap. He sticks his head in. Six egg rolls, four beers, a pack of shrimp chips, multicolored like confetti.

"The chips are for you," says Julie. "And I'm only having two egg rolls. I swear. I'm dieting."

"You *have* lost weight," says David.

"Eighteen pounds. Twelve to go. It's easy, you just drink one eight-ounce glass of water before every meal."

"I don't have any eight-ounce glasses."

"Too bad."

David pinches the full moon, clowning. They eat with the TV on, and play Chinese checkers, one game after another. Across the bright star shape of the checker board, they tell each other stories. Julie tells him about the time she got locked for an hour in a rest room at a gas station in Tennessee, and he tells her how, without meaning to, he had lied to Mandy about the hitchhiker. As usual, their separate entrapments seem complementary, and David wonders if all old friends feel like this or if the two of them are lucky. In bed he pulls Julie on top of him, to feel her diminished weight, and she plays up to it, enjoying herself, arching away from him, holding herself at arm's length. She is like a balloon, floating above him and then touching down.

"I was hoping to meet this Mandy," she says to him later.

"You can see her if you look out the window in the morning, when she goes to work."

But in the morning, gulping her mugs of water, Julie explains that she is getting serious with Seth, really serious, and that he and she are moving to Vermont to buy a house and start a bed and breakfast place.

"He's a great cook," she says, "and I don't mind cleaning up if I'm paid. We want to ski our lives away. You can stay there sometime."

David is surprised. It is as if she is at once on the brink of a slope, the poles tapping the snowy crust, teasing, so that the skis inch forward just enough to send her flying.

"I didn't know you skied," he says.

"I'll learn. But don't think it's so sudden—it's not, we've been talking about it for a year already."

"Has Seth stopped smoking yet?"

"When I lose thirty pounds."

"Then what happens when you gain it back? I can't picture you in a bed and breakfast, Julie."

"Neither can I." She kisses him, a long kiss, a good-bye kiss.

"There's something that's been happening," Mandy is saying, "that makes me think I might really be crazy."

She takes a long, nervous sip of her wine, and for a moment her hair falls over her face. David has to nudge her before she'll continue. Wine glasses in hand, they are skirting the reservoir, following the narrow path around its perimeter, detouring here and there because the high school kids are out, in clusters on the steep grassy edge, partying. A boy grunts in the bushes, and one girl wretches while two others stroke her back, all three of them laughing because its so new to them— drunken feelings, night air, freedom, space. In the morning, beer cans will float in the water, and cigarette butts, and someone's sweater on the rocks like a puddle of wool.

"For instance I'll be coming to a door, about to open it," Mandy explains, "any door, like a broom closet, because I have to sweep, or even the medicine cabinet, when I'm getting aspirin out, and before I open it I get this flash, this image of myself screaming, a horror movie scream, because there's something horrible on the other side of the door, it doesn't matter what, but what matters is I'm screaming for that split second in my mind, and I can feel it welling up, like I really want to scream, like I need to do it."

"Primal scream therapy, maybe."

"No, because it's private. It's not the scream that's important, it's the need. There was a girl in college who used to do it. A messy girl. She'd be walking along and then all at once she'd stop, and stand up straight and just wail, like a siren. But I could never do that, in public."

"That's self-control. You're sane, not crazy."

"I know it. I'm too sane. If I wasn't sane I wouldn't be with Eric anymore, I'd be with you."

"Anyone would have to be crazy to go out with me."

"Cut it out. I mean, even when I hate him, objectively I know I still love him. I do. I want to marry him and get it over with. I'm telling him that, tonight."

"What is it, my weight?"

"Stop joking, David. People like fat, they just won't admit it. And who knows what might have happened if you'd actually *done* something one of these nights. That's what Eric keeps saying: when the hell is David going to put the moves on you?"

"Everything you talk about always comes right back around to Eric," David says when they've circled the water. The pale shapes of the sycamores parallel the street, close together like the trees on the edge of a forest, except there isn't any forest, only darkness and square, damp lawns.

"Sorry," Mandy says, laughing. It's her laughter that conceals him when he reaches for her wrist, but she misinterprets, and hands the wine glass over, still half-full. Her door is locked, and she doesn't have a key. She checks under the mat. Nothing. She knocks on the door. Eric answers, wrapped up in a blanket, bleary-eyed. He gives David a courteous little bow.

"Night," Mandy calls, as she trips up the steps on her precarious heels, playing drunk, and disappears. In the glass in David's hand is a yellow star reflected from her bare kitchen bulb, blinking fiercely in the wine. He swallows it fast, before she turns out the light.

Fate and the Poet

He was a poet when she knew him. He carried a tooled leather briefcase containing his manuscripts, wherever he went. On the inside cover of the briefcase was pasted a slip of paper on which he had typed his address and phone number, and beneath that an urgent message: "This briefcase contains valuable manuscripts. *Please* return promptly. No questions asked. Reward."

He admitted to some discomfort over the use of the term "valuable," and later he added a few more lines. *"Valuable to me. Not to anyone else. Sentimental Value."*

Of course, the possibility remained that someone, upon finding his treasure, might send the poems to some literary magazines and publish them. He confessed to having nightmares about this. In the dream he would be flipping through the pages of a journal and would come upon one of his poems, imperfected, misspaced, the words he had intended to rearrange still in their original, blundering order. And on the page, of course, the name of the thief, and maybe a photograph, someone lipping a pipe, a wall of dog-eared books rising out of sight behind him. Or worse, an entire book of poems, winner of the Yale Younger Poets Award. The National Book Award. The American Book Critics Circle Award. The thief would be invited to read from the book on college campuses. Naturally, the poems would be read incorrectly, the stress all wrong, the rhythm, the pace, the meanings altered and destroyed. Her lover would have no recourse. But he enjoyed these dreams. He emerged from them shiny with sweat, his lips moist, the edges of his teeth gleaming with saliva, his entire body flushed with heat and desire. Frequently on these afternoons, in the very midst of lovemaking, he would pause while a look of delight swept over his face, and then when they were finished he would hurry, still naked and dripping, for the typewriter perched on the desk at the foot of the bed, where he would record whatever phrase had occurred to him prior to orgasm.

In public, in restaurants or in parks, sometimes on the sidewalk itself, he might stop what he was doing and open the briefcase to leaf through the layers of onionskin, in search of a particular image or passage whose exact cadence he had forgotten. Light fell through the paper as he held it up to read from it; from behind she could make out the shape of the poem, the way, as he put it, words moved along the page. Some were small and compact, like objects. Others appeared to have been tossed by a careless hand and allowed to sift, word by word, into haphazard place.

"There is no such thing as carelessness," he would say, offended. "The trick is to make it *look* unplanned, like an accident, when really everything matters."

He would not allow her to read them. A poem needs to be read in *print,* he insisted, in a book or a magazine. Otherwise, it might appear incomplete, unfinished, raw, undigested, premature. He used all of these words, at one time or another, and when she still failed to understand, he compared the reading of an unpublished poem to those clipped previews of feature films you see in movie theaters before the show—the viewer is left unsatisfied, with conflicting expectations and confused emotions. She once told him she thought he was merely protecting himself, but he got so angry, so silent and mean, that the accusation wasn't worth pursuing. He did allow her, however, to read from the draft of a novel he was writing. The novel, he said, was a hobby. In the first pages of the book, an outlaw entered a saloon, threw some coins on the bar, downed three shots of whiskey, and complained to the bartender that his woman made him use a rubber all the time and that he never felt anything.

"When does this take place?" she asked him. "I mean, the settings are Old West but the dialogue is modern."

"It's a rough draft," he said. "It's just something I'm doing in my spare time."

They were seniors at a university in St. Louis. He was older, having worked two years in New Orleans. Something to do with boats, docks, loading. Also, he had learned how to pilot an airplane. He wore a heavy leather jacket and a frayed silk scarf. If, while they were walking, a private plane flew overhead, he squinted into the sky to follow its path.

She had a husband. He was gentle and intelligent, a graduate student, with an unruly beard that she trimmed now and then with a nail scissors. That was what came to mind when she thought of him—her own, tender ministrations, his chin cupped in the palm of her hand, the curled black hairs falling from between the twin blades of the miniature scissors. When she was done, she patted the front of his flannel shirt so the stray hairs floated to the bathroom floor. Then she swept, and her husband held the dustpan while she whisked the hairs into it.

They lived in married student housing, in an apartment with too few windows. On the walls she had taped a series of botanical illustrations torn month by month from a calendar, each matted on a sheet of construction paper whose color emphasized a hint of color hidden in the drawing. Most often, the color resided in the sexual parts of the flower—the pistil, the anthers, the shadowy recesses where the petals fused.

Her husband had seen the calendar in a bookstore and bought it for her. Very quickly it became her most valued possession. She grew impatient for the end of each month, when she could tear off the preceding page to reveal a new one. The drawings had been made by monks during the nineteenth century; she liked to imagine the silent, balding men in their simple robes, gathering herbs in a forest and then returning to their rooms to sketch them. With a feather pen. By candlelight. Pressing her face to these flowers, she smelled earth, sweat, and incense. She felt close to the monks, as if she knew them by name. Did monks have names? They seemed fatherly and safe, bodiless, untroubled by the excesses of human emotions. In a way, she envied them. Mornings, drinking from a mug of hot coffee, she circled the rooms and examined the drawings for details she might not have noticed—the speck of pollen on the stigma, the bumblebee, the drop of moisture on the underside of a leaf. Each appealed to her with the force of a revelation. She pointed them out to her husband, who seemed genuinely charmed by her enthusiasm. She did not point them out to her lover, who never came to the house and didn't know about the calendar. In her imagination, the monks had slaved over each drawing for her sake and for the sake of her husband, to cement their marriage, and to compensate for the ordinariness of their lives together. It frightened her that at the end of the year, when the last page had been torn from the calendar, she might not find another to replace it.

Her lover's name was Larry Oliver. He was proud of this name; it suited his calling. On the top of the pile of poems in his briefcase was a single sheet of onionskin with the name typed in caps in the center of it; it looked melodious and graceful, like a careful arrangement of musical notes. He was a vain man, most eager to please himself. He liked to fluster his superiors, the teachers at the university, by blurting out, mid-lecture, a series of disarming and challenging questions that entertained the other students. Then he would lean back in his seat and smile patiently as the lecturer struggled to regain his composure. "You seem to think you have earned the right to be difficult," one of his professors wrote on a paper. "And the odd thing is, you *have*." He tacked the note to the wall in his bedroom. He told her lengendary anecdotes that dramatized the difficult natures of other poets, famous ones. Theodore Roethke, for instance, who was a drunk and a fighter. James Dickey, who blasted obscene comments from the podium every time he gave a reading. Robert Frost, who, legend had it, once set fire to a barn. Most of all, he liked the story of a poet named Frank O'Hara, who lay down on a beach, dozed off, and got run over by a jeep.

"What does that have to do with being difficult?" she said. She was puzzled and horrified. It was late afternoon, November, darkness had fallen. Earlier, she had watched him sprinkle seed on the fire escape, for some blackbirds.

"It's enigmatic," he said, pleased with himself. "You don't think it was an accident, do you?"

"Of course, it must have been," she argued. "How could he have known the jeep was coming?"

"He *knew*."

On the bed was a patchwork quilt that a prior girl friend had made for him. For a little while she marveled over the swirls of minute, even stitching, a pattern so complex as to be nearly invisible. She had seen this girl on campus, a small, pretty, blonde girl in a camel's hair coat, and she suspected that the poet still loved her in secret.

"You still love Jeanne, don't you?" she said, because she didn't want to talk about a man getting run over by a jeep. But the poet didn't answer. He got up and found her underthings and handed them to her. He would watch her as she dressed. When she was fully clothed, he would still be naked. That was the image she had of him—standing naked and pale in the middle of the room as she zipped up her coat. Nothing ever made him uncomfortable. Sometimes, when she left, he would be picking a piece of lint from the hair on his testicles. Other times, he would follow her out through the kitchen, find himself an orange, and stand naked at the window, peeling it, as she made her way down to the street. He lived in a rotten part of University City, and often she felt frightened walking home. Everything was gray—the sidewalks, the faces of the buildings, the bare trees, the windowpanes and the automobiles. In her blue jeans she felt conspicuous. What if her husband were to see her? But what would he be doing here? He was not the kind of man who frequented the bars on Delmar Avenue. In fact, he led a marvelously placid and circumscribed existence, leaving the apartment in the mornings, following the ginkgo-lined pathways to the laboratory, lunching in the cafeteria with a few other graduate students from his own department, and then, in the evenings, walking home along another path that skirted the road, so he could stop at the corner and buy a newspaper. He never breakfasted. He barely left the confines of the campus. He was loyal to the life that seemed to have been chosen for him, never complaining, never bored, content with the present. In this way, she supposed, he resembled a dog, one of those good-looking dogs that trotted purposefully around and then returned home for its supper. She loved him, sometimes, the way she might love such a dog—affectionately, hopelessly. He was dependable. He worked with methyl salicylate, preparing turtle cells for study under a microscope. At night, he smelled of wintergreen.

The idea of leaving her husband was not an impossible one. She entertained it at times, but it always seemed unlikely and abstract, like the thought of parachuting from an airplane. On Sunday mornings, lounging in bed with the comics, her husband spoke as longingly of their future as if he were reminiscing about their past. He would complete his dissertation, find a job in a college town. They would buy a house, have a child. If the child were a girl they might name her Madeleine, after his mother, who was dead. But what if it were a boy?

"Larry," she said once, testing him.

"That's okay," he said. "But the real name would have to be Lawrence and I don't like the name Lawrence, do you?"

They would find her a job, maybe something in the library at the college where he worked, and eventually she might return to school to pursue whatever interested her. But she wouldn't have to, not if she didn't want to. She might open a boutique or become a caterer who worked privately out of her home and stayed close to the children.

"But I can't cook," she said.

"Whatever," said her husband. "Whatever you want."

Then he would put the funny pages aside and they would

make careful love to one another. What gratified her most was the way their two bodies seemed simply to fuse together, necessarily, like two drops of water on a windowpane. She was on the pill. If she forgot to take one, he reminded her. He seemed somehow to sense her lapses and distractions without needing to know what caused them. He tended to her as if she were a plant that experienced peculiar cycles of flowering and withdrawal.

After lovemaking they showered, separately. Washing, she allowed herself to think of what her life might be like if she were to spend it with the poet. She envisioned her lover careening through space and through time, herself hanging on or charging after him in wild pursuit, her hair uncombed, the bills unpaid, falling breathlessly on top of him in bed after bed in a long line of furnished apartments, burdened only by the weight of his ancient Smith Corona. Where would they live? Africa. France. New Guinea. New Mexico. When they had money they would spend it with abandon. When they didn't, they wouldn't miss it. He wouldn't want children. He needed "to be free." They would never marry. Well, maybe in old age. But by then he would be dead, she was certain, killed in a small plane crash or during one of his crazy exploits, eaten by a lion, shot by a firing squad in some undeveloped country. She would ship him home to bury him, her suitcase crammed with obituary clippings ringing with praise for his numerous published works. But she would be the only person at the funeral. In the end, she might assemble a small volume of "posthumous poems in progress," including several disclaimers, apologies, her own well-meant attempts at editing.

The poet got a letter one afternoon. She heard it fall through the mail slot to the floor in his living room—an urgent swish, like an intake of breath. He was sleeping. Asleep, his face assumed the contours of a child's face, smooth but somehow blurred, as if the features had been filtered through a layer of peace. Just to look at him you wouldn't guess he was so talented a lover. He was small, delicate, blonde. In bed he was energetic, magnificent really. Maybe he had read that book, that bestseller, *How to Make Love to a Woman*. She had searched for it once on his shelves but hadn't found it. There were poetry books, critical anthologies, biographies, journals, and crowding the edges of the shelves a collection of wonderful objects. Shells. Carvings. Small stone pipes and empty bottles. Candles. Restaurant ashtrays. A tray of matchbooks. A ceramic bowl filled with unstrung beads composed of a material that she could not identify—pearly in color, smooth as teeth, but when she scratched one with her fingernail a white, chalky substance appeared underneath it. He was a sensuous man. These were all things you wanted to touch when you looked at them.

She watched him sleep, and listened to the smooth, relaxed pace of his breathing. But she could not dull her awareness of the letter in the other room. Finally she climbed out of bed and went into the living room to look at it, wrapping his robe around her. There it was, the neat white rectangle of paper, lying at an angle on the floor. She picked it up and scanned the address. The handwriting was a woman's, a precise, looping script. And on the other side, a local address, and the name of the girl who had sewn the quilt.

She did not wake her lover. She dressed in silence, put the letter in her pocket, and left the apartment.

Then, hurrying through the dusky streets, she saw a van drive past and then stop and back up. The driver honked and rolled down the window on the passenger side. Would she like a ride? Barely glancing at him, she shook her head no and kept walking, suddenly nervous. She buried her chin in her coat collar and stared ahead at the sidewalk. Years earlier, as a child, she was approached by a man in a large, pale blue car, who offered to drive her the few blocks to her house. She said no, as she had been trained to do. At home, she related this small but important event to her mother, who stood at the window, picking at the fiber of the curtains. Now she thought of all the women murdered by strange men in strange cities, in the backs of vans. Where would he have taken her, to dispose of her? She thought of Forest Park—the bike trail in the woods, abandoned in winter, and of the small ponds shadowed by willows. Maybe they would find her, maybe they wouldn't. Maybe in the spring: a bicyclist, stopping to admire some ducks in the pond, sees a hand poking out of the water, pale white, muddied, on the third finger the glint of a wedding band. Or maybe the murderer had made off with the ring, had chopped off the finger—after she was dead, of course—removed the ring, wrapped it in a handkerchief, and pawned it. They would find the soggy letter in her pocket, and trace it to her lover, who would become a prime suspect in the case. Traces of his frozen sperm would be discovered inside of her. He would be tried, convicted, imprisoned. Would he have access to a typewriter? But her husband would be satisfied. She imagined him alone in a smaller apartment (no longer eligible for married student housing), fixing his dinner, reading the paper, sleeping, waking, walking to work, walking home, his unvarying habits left intact along with a new one, the habit of grief, which he accepted tamely as he did the others.

Remorsefully, she walked more quickly, eager to be home when he got there. But at the sight of the overpass that would take her to the university she paused, bewildered. She hadn't looked at the driver, had she? Maybe he was someone she knew, who knew her. After all, that part of the city provided cheap living for students. Maybe the driver had been a student, a graduate student, a graduate student in her husband's department, a friend of her husband's, who recognized her, who would mention to her husband that his wife was taking chances, walking alone in the dark in that part of the city, refusing his offer of a safe trip home. At dinner one night, her husband would ask, "But what were you doing *there?*"

She would need to have an answer on hand. Of course, it would be better to anticipate the question, to provide him with the answer before he had to ask. She turned around and ran five blocks back into the city, to a bakery she knew would be open. But she had no money. She ran to her lover's and banged on the door until he opened it. He was eating his dinner. It was nearly six o'clock. "I need money!" she said. "A few dollars. I can't explain!" He grinned, and unfolded some money from his wallet and gave it to her. At the bakery, she bought a loaf of braided bread sprinkled with poppy seeds, and two small dessert tortes. She held the warm package close to her body as she ran. The sky was black, the moon was out. Her husband was cooking hamburgers when she got to him. "I bought this to surprise you," she said to him. "I'm sorry I'm late. I thought you would like these." She nearly believed what she said. She gave him the package. "Thanks!" said her husband. He kissed her, and together they sliced up the bread and ate.

Later, after dinner, she went into the bathroom and locked the door. Her husband was on the telephone with another graduate student, discussing a gel he had run on some turtle cells. She could tell he was excited, in that calm way he had, pausing briefly here and there as he spoke, tapping the eraser of his pencil on the spine of a textbook. She tried to match his composure. By poking the sharp point of the nail scissor beneath the flap of the envelope, she was able to open it without causing any damage. The letter was short, typed on sturdy blue paper. She was shocked that it was typed—it resembled a fragment of poetry. It read:

> I'm pregnant.
> I love you.
> Jeanne.

Of course, she had intended to reseal the letter, with rubber cement, and to drop it in his mail slot one day when she knew he would be in class. But she couldn't. She tore it into pieces and flushed it down the toilet along with a small amount of urine.

She told herself she did this to save him—he was in love with Jeanne, he would allow her to come back into his life and destroy it. They would have the baby, settle down. He would put his poetry aside and find a steady, paying job. He would work his way up, becoming the manager of one of those chain bookstores he despised. She had a vision of him shining his shoes before going to work, neglecting to wipe the polish from his hands before kissing the baby good-bye, leaving, on the baby's diaper, a brown smudge that he would mistake for excrement. He would make himself late for work, changing the baby's diaper and puzzling over the fact that it was still fresh and clean. Eventually, to coincide with the birth of a second child, he would enroll in night school, in business administration. In the bookstore, passing the shelves of new poetry books with their slender, multicolored spines, he would avert his gaze. He would hate himself.

When she saw him again, she was giddy. He interpreted the giddiness as passion. That month, she got her period earlier than usual. Her husband didn't like to make love to her when she was bleeding, but the poet didn't mind. Afterward, she would look at her blood on him and imagine she had done something terrible to wound him.

On campus, she found herself searching for Jeanne, for the small camel's hair coat and the fake leather boots that looked elegant but inexpensive. At last, on the first of December, she came across her in the snack bar, holding, with both hands, a half-pint of milk, sipping it through a straw. Sitting alone at the large, round table, with her books and coat and pocketbook piled on the other chairs, Jeanne looked smaller than ever, pale and thoughtful. Her nose was red. It was cold outside, or maybe she had been crying. On her tray was the crust of a sandwich and a packet of tissues. When she stood up to go, she did not look pregnant. But she had trouble with her coat; the sleeves of her sweater bunched up when she tried to put it on, so she had to take it off again and grab the ends of the sleeves with her fingers. Then she put on her gloves, fake leather that matched her boots. But she looked so graceful! What would become of her? When she left, the room seemed suddenly to grow noisier.

Several years later, in Virginia, in the small, pleasant college town where both she and her husband are teaching, she finds herself talking with a friend, a woman whose life is remarkably similar to her own, and she surprises herself by explaining to this friend the details of her love affair with the poet, how it began, progressed, stalled, and ended finally when they both left St. Louis. What surprises her most is the disparaging tone of her own voice, her ironical assessment of the poet's love-making abilities. He was perfect, she says. "But too perfect. As if he'd read everything in a manual, like painting by numbers, like he was reading my mind, because he always knew exactly what I needed, when to start, when to stop, what felt good, what didn't, what felt great. After a while it all began to seem very mechanical, like he was some kind of genius robot. Do you know what I'm saying?"

But her friend does not. Fixed on her face is a puzzled expression, the beginnings of a mistrustful smile. She offers tea. They brew some and drink, staring into their cups in silence. The friend's husband is a linguist, and the friend herself is a lecturer in the Spanish department, where she is a graduate student. The four of them work hard at what they do, too hard maybe, holed up in their separate offices, their four typewriters clacking. They joke that they live like monks, working even on Saturday nights, sharing, at two in the morning, their hot pots of coffee. In summer, when the other couple leaves town, she writes them letters, typing on the backs of the monks' drawings, which she has stored in a trunk because the edges are torn and they are fading. Oddly, the very last one, the one from the month of December, is her favorite, a simple watercolor, Jefferson Plum. The twin globes of burnished fruit hang from a fragment of twig adorned with ordinary leaves. And the background is depthless, a flat, stony gray. The sight of the fruit hanging in the center of it suggests nothing but a perishable loveliness in the face of blankness. It still makes her think of Jeanne. Whatever happened to her? And the poet, what happened to him?

When they parted, he was flourishing. He had mailed some poems to a literary magazine and they had been rejected. "Those pinheads," he kept saying. "Those worthless pieces of junk they publish."

Still she scans the tables of contents in the literary magazines, as well as the *Books in Print Author Index,* for her ex-lover's name. One day, she finds the name Larry Oliver, but the book is a mathematical treatise with an impossible title. She orders it anyway, through interlibrary loan. There is no picture on the flap, which means it couldn't be the poet's, who wouldn't publish a book without his picture on it. And its pages are filled with outlandish equations. When she brings it home, her husband discovers it. "What are you doing with this?" he asks. "One of my students left it in class," she says, and she takes the book away from him abruptly as if it might betray her.

She has learned to admire, even to enjoy, her husband's quiet, easy style of lovemaking—his patient need, his attentive gaze, his subdued adoration of her body. Clearly, he intends to please her, so she is pleased. She thinks of time-lapse photography, the gentle unfolding of a bud into flower. And he is capable, too, of surprising her. He has been asked to write a book about turtles; he has accepted the offer. "I can take a sabbatical," he explains. "We can go somewhere. We may as well go somewhere interesting. Where would you like to go?"

"Tahiti," she says.

He believes her. "We'll need access to libraries," he says. "An English-speaking country would be best. Or we could stay in the U.S. There are so many parts of this country I'd like to see. We could go to the Pacific Northwest. Or New England. You can finish writing there. We could live in London! We have to think about this!"

"Yes," she says. She doesn't know what to think. She thinks of sailing round the world on a houseboat, but she doesn't know if such a thing is possible. And she imagines the two of them settling in a foreign city while continuing to live exactly as they did in Virginia—walking to the library, walking home, making do with a primitive kitchen. Maybe, she thinks, she should not take her husband seriously. He will never follow through with such a plan. He will lose heart at the very last minute and they will have to cancel all of their arrangements. But she is patient with him, and when he returns from town with an armload of travel brochures she takes the night off to look through them, exclaiming with him over the pictures.

Several months go by and the two of them, engrossed in their work, forget to mention the sabbatical. She feels responsible for this, afraid that her husband has sensed her reluctance. He is careful with her. He buys her another calendar. But this is a wilderness calendar, filled with photographs of wildflowers, and the slick, bright images fail to interest her. In fact, just looking at them makes her miserable. She becomes distracted. She blames her distraction on the gift. Daily, she phones her friend, the Spanish instructor, and complains that she can't concentrate. So when finally she comes upon the poet's name, in the alumni magazine from the university they went to, she is unprepared. At first, she skims past it without recognition. Then, later, folding up the magazine to stuff it into the garbage, she pauses, reopens it, skims it again. Larry Oliver, she reads, lives in Boston with his wife, Monique, and their two children. He is a market analyst.

How many times does she read this? She sits down at the table with a cup of coffee and the magazine open before her. Monique, she repeats. The name is French. She imagines a slim, fashionable woman with feathery hair and no English. Perhaps he has learned to speak French. But the children, of course, are bilingual, if they are talking yet at all. Perhaps they are twins. She imagines two infants, swaddled in disposable diapers, each with a rosebud mouth pressed noisily to one of Monique's perfect breasts.

"So tell me," says her husband, as she is climbing into bed with him one night, "what you are thinking."

He has begun, recently, to play this game with her. "What are you thinking?" he will ask. "Nothing," she always says, because of course he only asks when he knows she is thinking of nothing, when she is sweeping the floor, or washing dishes, or fooling with the dial on the radio. She likes this game—it is playful, a private joke.

Now she looks at him, smiling. His beard needs a trimming. In the glow from the reading lamp several clumps of hair stick out in all directions. She turns off the lamp.

"I was thinking," she says, "about taking our sabbatical in Boston." She kisses him hard on the mouth.

Nuns in Love

On her way home from work Cynthia passes a convent surrounded by a high brick wall interspersed with locked gates. Through the parallel bars of these gates she can see the rather drab, unimpressive convent grounds and a building nestled in evergreen trees. With its flat roof and rows of plate glass windows, it resembles an office building; on the dull rainy days of this season a fluorescent glow emanates from behind the glass. Placed along some walkways are several slatted wood benches that no one ever seems to sit on, and in the flower beds are shrubs instead of flowers, miniature shrubs with flattened tops. Pigeons march throughout, staining the walks and benches with their droppings.

There are few nuns to be seen on the convent grounds, but this is to be expected—nuns are by nature reclusive. Besides, the gates are widely spaced and offer only glimpses of the goings-on behind the wall. Cynthia once heard laughter rising from the other side of it, a high peal of laughter like the shriek of a hyena, but there was no way of knowing for certain whether the laughter came from a nun. She imagines that the nuns spend most of their time indoors, performing scholarly duties or other activities of a routine nature, always thinking about God and about how much they love him. She does not know which confuses her more, the notion of God, or the notion of love, or the notion of loving God. All three seem impossible, burdens that no girl in her right mind would inflict upon herself.

This afternoon Cynthia sees two nuns coming toward her on the sidewalk. One is sitting in a wheelchair that the other is pushing, but both are young and animated, with bright rosy faces. In their eager conversation they appear not to notice her. Just as Cynthia steps off the sidewalk to avoid bumping into them, soaking her sneaker in a puddle, the nuns stop abreast of a gate to slide a laminated identification card into a metal box. The gate opens noiselessly and the nuns pass through it. Cynthia watches as they wheel down the walkway between the stunted gardens, shooing pigeons with their skirts. Tonight she tells her new friend Richard about the two nuns, embellishing them for the sake of entertainment. In her story the nun in the wheelchair wore rainbow-striped socks with toes.

"At least I think they were socks," she ad-libs. "I couldn't see that far up. It's possible they were hose."

Richard, with a look of pained humor as if the thought of a nun in panty hose embarrasses him, gazes at her over his fondue pot. Ever since she met him, just three weeks ago, he has tried to impress her with ingenious and elaborate meals; tonight there's a platter of neat cubed beef and six ceramic bowls, each filled with a sauce of a different color. With a long-handled fork he demonstrates how the beef is speared and then allowed to cook in boiling oil.

"Don't eat it directly out of the pot," he warns. "Slide it off the fork, and then when it's cooled a little use this other fork to eat it with. Otherwise you'll burn your mouth."

Cynthia finds the entire process captivating and affected, much like Richard himself. There is about him an air of inconsequential refinement—his rooms are clean, cream-colored, and suffused with a vacant airy quality that is like the absence of gravity, as if they might cease to exist entirely if no one was sitting in them. In truth, the contrast between her own messy life and the careful, spare arrangements of Richard's days is a comfort to her. He is the kind of man who buys for his coffee table books intended exclusively for that purpose, and each evening while he pours the coffee Cynthia sits herself down in the living room and opens one of them. Tonight's book is called *Labyrinths.* Its pages are covered with pen and ink drawings of beautiful and complex mazes which Cynthia immediately attempts to solve. She finds in her purse a green felt tip marker and begins to make her way through the mazes, abandoning each one the minute she finds herself stuck. Richard is horrified to see that she is actually drawing on the pages of his expensive book.

"What ..." he says. "You're not supposed to ... Oh, well."

Cynthia sighs. As if ignorant of Richard's presence and of the coffee cup he is holding out to her, she continues wrecking the book with her pen. This particular maze takes place in the innards of an elaborately rendered unicorn and seems to lead from the mouth to the anus, or from the anus to the mouth, depending on where you go in. Cynthia traces a route through the coil of the unicorn's intestines, only to find herself mired in the stomach cavity with no means of escape.

"This would be a perfectly nice book," she says, "except for these stupid mazes. None of them go anywhere."

Richard opens his mouth like a fish. For three weeks Cynthia has been aware of his gigantic desire to get into bed with her. He once confessed to her exactly how much time had elapsed since he had slept with a woman, and she responded with a sincere astonishment that agitated him. Thinking back, she remembers having felt for him a vague, automatic attraction, the same she might have felt for any man who was attentive to her and polite enough and not bad looking, but the feeling had no staying power. Since then, she has fallen into the habit of teasing him and has lost sight of her own intentions. Now, as he sips his coffee, she places the blunt end of her marker between her lips and begins toying with it, circling it with the tip of her tongue. She slips her shoes off and pulls her feet up underneath her. Richard leans forward in his chair and clasps and unclasps his hands.

"Cynthia," he says finally. "May I touch you?"

"Sure," she says.

Richard gets up, circles the coffee table, positions himself next to her, places his hands on her shoulders, and pulls her to him. He is trembling.

"Not *now*," says Cynthia, focusing on him a look of sympathy and exasperation. "You have to learn to be spontaneous. You have to learn to do things without always talking about them first."

Richard looks stunned and dejected.

"That's not what you said the last time," he says. "You said not to jump right into things. You said you needed to be prepared."

"That was last time," says Cynthia. She continues sucking on the pen. Her mouth tastes of ink—sharp and metallic, the flavor of power. After a minute she stands, allowing the book of mazes to slide from her lap onto his. The pages fan apart like the petals of a flower and then fall together with a whisper.

On the following day, a Saturday, Cynthia sees a nun wearing striped socks under her habit. The stripes are all colors of the rainbow and the five toes of each foot are separate, allowing the straps of the nun's thongs to fit between them. The day is fine, damp and sunny. Since everybody seems to be coming out of the woodwork, it is perhaps not surprising that the nun should be outside too, where she can easily be seen, adjacent to a set of gates, hoeing a small portion of earth vigorously. In fact Cynthia is feeling so busy and distracted by the fury of activity on the streets, by the cyclists, the Frisbees, the wash on the lines, the dog walkers, that she might not have noticed the nun if not for those socks and the way their bright horizontal stripes stood out against the square of dark fresh-turned earth. She stops abruptly when she sees them, wide-eyed, remembering at once all the rainbows she has ever seen and the feeling of cynicism and disbelief she had when she saw them, as if rainbows were a joke being played on her. On the nun's face is a look of blissful concentration like the look of a person admiring a loved one. Her eyes are blurred, her brow smooth, her lips pursed as if for a kiss. Noticing Cynthia peering at her through the bars of the gate, she smiles. Cynthia jumps, startled, and resumes her walk with blank determination, street after street, lot after lot, along a highway overpass, down a steep embankment studded with dandelions, across the highway into one strange neighborhood after another, into the suburbs where people are washing their cars, and then out of the middle-class suburbs and into the rich ones. Two teenaged boys on a motorcycle whiz by then make a U-turn and offer her a ride.

"I'm supposed to sit on the handlebars, right?" says Cynthia. The two boys nod and gawk at her as if she were naked.

"No thanks," says Cynthia. "I'll pass. Where am I, anyway?"

"Ladue," says one of the boys. "Fortunoff's right down the street. Over that way." He points with his dirty hand and then nudges the other boy, who after a second climbs down from the cycle to offer her his seat. She accepts, shrugging, and wraps her arms around the driver.

"You going to Fortunoff's?" he asks, then guns the motor and starts off before she answers him. The sad boy stands in the center of the road, on an island of grass, and watches them go. They turn down an avenue overhung with plane trees and follow it to a parking lot. In the center of the lot is the department store lit with yellow bulbs, and only at this moment does Cynthia realize that dusk has fallen and that the air is chilly. As the boy slows the cycle for a turn, she hops from the seat and feels in her pockets for change. In Fortunoff's she telephones Richard, who sounds far away.

"I hitched a ride to Fortunoff's," she tells him. "Now I'm stuck."

"In Ladue!" says Richard. "What are you doing there?"

"Just looking. Shopping around. Only I'm broke."

"I'll buy you whatever you want," Richard says when he arrives. He is wearing his white shirt and white slacks and white socks and white shoes, the same outfit he was wearing when Cynthia first met him, in the supermarket around the corner from her building. Its spotlessness astounded her then and astounds her now, so that she finds herself looking for stains, around the collar and the waistband, wherever a stain might escape notice, only there aren't any.

"I don't want anything," she says.

Finally Richard selects a one-cup porcelain drip coffee maker and several imported dish towels, elegant but practical. He seems proud of his purchase but subdued, as if something is troubling him. In the car he says, "I didn't know you hitched. You shouldn't. It's dangerous and stupid."

"It wasn't dangerous," says Cynthia. "I got a ride with a nun. I felt like driving around. Now I'm starving."

"Okay. Dinner. Where to?"

They end up in a crepe place with candles on the tables. The waitresses wear blue and white checked aprons over miniskirts.

"I don't think I've ever seen you in a skirt," says Richard. "I thought girls were supposed to be wearing skirts again."

"I have chicken legs," Cynthia tells him.

"Nonsense. I bet they're beautiful." Richard reaches across the table and takes hold of one of Cynthia's wrists and turns it over in his palm and strokes with his free hand the tracery of blue veins on the soft underside of her arm. Cynthia has never mentioned to him that her arms are a remarkably sensitive part of her body and that the merest touch is pleasurable. She leans back and half closes her eyes. After a minute she extends the other arm and asks Richard to please stroke that one too. His expression changes when she says this, becoming dead serious, and he fixes on her that steady, wicked manly gaze that is popular in movies. When the waitress brings the crepes, he spears a morsel with his fork and offers it wordlessly. Cynthia takes the food into her mouth. It seems that everyone in the restaurant is watching. In the heady, winy silence, Cynthia makes up a story about the nun who drove her to Fortunoff's. The nun was driving a tiny red convertible, she explains to Richard. In the passenger seat was a sheep dog that Cynthia had to take on her lap. The nun's headdress flew out behind them as they sped between the rows of plane trees, and droplets of the sheep dog's spittle made a fine warm rain on Cynthia's face.

After dinner, in the car, Richard presses his face against her neck and chest and begins whispering things. Cynthia is chilly and her nipples are erect; Richard bites them through the grainy cloth of her T-shirt. The parking lot is dark all around but sometimes cars pull in and out.

"Not *here*," Cynthia finally says, barely able to hear herself above the storm of Richard's breathing. "This is a parking lot. I'm not ... I can't ..."

Richard pulls himself away and starts the car and drives home with frenzied impatient maneuvers that seem designed to scare the other drivers off the road. He leads her up the sidewalk to the door of his apartment, where for a minute it seems he has misplaced his key. In the living room they press against one another and sway back and forth on their feet.

"Let me take off your shirt," Richard says.

He guides her ahead of him into the bedroom. In the bedroom is a door with a window in it.

"What is this?" asks Cynthia. "Where does it go?"

She opens the door and steps through it into the sudden cool of the night air.

"Stop!" says Richard.

But she ducks away and hurries home without him, through an alley and past the bakery where in the window the cakes are lit like planets.

Several days later, crossing an intersection just north of the cleaners where she works, Cynthia's attention is caught by the whine of tires and the appearance of a tiny red convertible that jumps a red light and continues up the hill in fitful jerks as if its clutch has disengaged. Sitting inside, close together like lovers on an outing, are a nun and a large white curly-haired dog with its tongue hanging out. Cynthia can see, in the rear-view mirror, that the nun is singing crazily along with the radio and that the sheep dog appears to be smiling.

Cynthia is transfixed.

At any rate she can find no other word for it, for this awful heightened sensibility into which she feels she has ascended, like a plane through clouds into thin air. She is just coming home from the cleaners, two rooms in a low-ceilinged building smelling of steam and lint and plastic wrapping; all day she ran clothes through a press and then for an hour searched the drawer of stray buttons for one missing from a lady's coat. Then she sewed it back on, with matching thread, a yellow button with yellow thread, while the lady tapped a nickel on the Formica top of the counter. Cynthia's feet ached and her hair grew limp; she kept thinking how it wouldn't hold a curl. Also of Richard. She would see him tonight, of course, and the next night and the next, and each night would be different from the last although somehow similar, or similar but somehow different. Last night he had revealed to her the notion of the sort of woman with whom he might like to spend the rest of his life; the woman, he confessed, need not be of any particular intelligence or beauty or talent or accomplishment. In fact the idea of a homely woman has begun to appeal to him, someone humble and simple and full of need. He dreams of a buck-toothed girl of impoverished background, dressed in a stiff-collared blouse and a skirt whose zipper jams whenever he undresses her, whose stockings are torn, who mends them with nail polish, who under her clothing is supple and urgent and surprisingly athletic.

Cynthia didn't know what to say to this or if she should even think about saying anything. This was not the first time that Richard had conjured a girl for himself, an unlikely girl who was, in various ways, the precise opposite of Cynthia herself. One had a small child and lots of money, one played flute in a symphony, one was Chinese and spoke with a lilt. Each he described with what seemed like true adoration as his thin face grew paler and shadowed, taking on the look of a man stranded on an island.

"I've named her," he said. "Paulette. I *need* her."

He turned back to his ice crusher, pressing a button. There was a noise like a traffic accident and then silence. He scooped the crushed ice into goblets whose rims had been frosted with salt. Margaritas. A Mexican meal. He was wearing a sombrero.

Cynthia thought to herself how naive he was, and how his na-
ivete made him innocent, and how his innocence entertained
her. She too had dressed up for the night, in velveteen trou-
sers and a transparent blouse; underneath it her nipples made
blonde shadows. Richard kept trying not to look at them. He
plucked a hard red pepper from a bunch of chilis hanging
from the ceiling, causing the bunch to shudder. A moth flew
out from among the chilis. Then another and another. They
were graceful and discreet as they flitted to the ceiling and
then floated back down, disappearing once again among the
red black hollows.

Richard didn't notice them. He was busy with the chili,
crushing it over a stew. Cynthia tapped the bunch of peppers
with her fingernail. Out flew more moths. She tapped harder.
They whirled about her.

"Look at this, Richard," she said.

"Just a second."

But when he turned to look, the moths had vanished.

"Look," Cynthia repeated. It was warm in the kitchen; she
unbuttoned the top of her blouse. Misunderstanding, Richard
stumbled toward her with his arms outstretched.

"Later," said Cynthia. "Not when I'm hungry." She pushed
him away, into the chilis, which fell clattering to the floor. A
cloud of white moths rose at once, obscuring them from one
another.

Now the nun in the sports car has vanished, leaving behind a
ribbon of sunlight on a hillside empty of traffic. Cynthia still
sees vividly the redness of the car and the black and whiteness
of the nun and the pinkness of the dog's tongue. She is thinking that the lies she tells Richard always come true, and that
this has to do with God, or that it has to do with love.

On a rainy day, at five o'clock, Richard surprises her by
showing up at the cleaners in his rain coat, ready to accom-
pany her home.

"A walk in the rain ..." he says, leaning with his elbow on the counter. He looks dreamy in his slick coat with the upturned collar, staring at Cynthia, spinning his umbrella while he waits. They take the road up the hill past the convent, where the rain beads up among the needles of the evergreens and cleanses the sidewalks and darkens the slatted wood benches. Beneath the benches, where the ground is drier, pigeons gather in little conversational groups.

"Rats with wings," says Richard.

"I've heard that before," says Cynthia, "but I've never agreed with it. I like pigeons."

"They have noble heads," says Richard. "I know what you mean. And the sounds they make."

"Cooing."

"Yes. And the colors."

"Purple and blue," says Cynthia. "Except for the black and white ones."

"And the reddish ones."

"Right," says Cynthia. She takes hold of his sleeve and they continue silently, because the purr of the rain on his umbrella seems to command silence. Walking beneath it, Cynthia feels they have entered a circle that is their life together. Richard's shined shoes creak as they go, and Cynthia's pink sneakers squelch and gurgle like something drowning. At the door to her apartment, she invites him inside, where he has never been. Laundry lies scattered throughout, the dirty mixed with the clean, and she tells him how she has to pick through it every morning, walking from room to room, looking for something to wear. Along the way, she admits, she clears the dishes and cups she finds sitting on the arms of chairs, sometimes swallowing the last muddy dregs of coffee before stacking the cups in the sink.

"I'm a mess," she exclaims. "A pig."

"I know that," says Richard. "Let's make love."

They begin to undress one another, surprised to find raindrops under their collars. Cynthia traces with her tongue the path of a raindrop along the flat white plane of his sternum, between the ribs. She is moved suddenly by the very bodiness of his body, the bones palpable under the skin, the skin itself, the hairs on its surface, the pores she can see if she gets close. This is what she loves—the surfaces of things, the purity of the surface of a man's body.

"Wait," she says, looking past his shoulder at the window. "There's a nun in a treetop, waving."

"Of course there is," says Richard. He lowers her onto the laundry on top of her bed, kissing her eyes shut before she has a chance to wave back.

The Habit of Friendship

Carla was one of those fat women whose sloppy children and houses attracted stray cats and nose colds along with other things in need of random resting places—wrong numbers, for instance, and overdue library books that no one recalled having read. She had a lot of friends, and I was one of them. My family moved around a lot in those days. My husband was in construction; he followed the jobs, and I followed him. I waitressed, or worked in shops, and had a small daughter to care for. My friendships with other women typically had about them a tentativeness common among the friendships of transients; we all took care not to like each other too much. But Carla's big tented figure seemed to vibrate with a generous and enfolding spirit. She wore giant striped-framed eyeglasses which actually looked, in a crazy way, nice on her, and her beautiful dimpled hands were of the tapered variety common in old-fashioned portraiture. But she was not old-fashioned. She was a lot like me, in the things that mattered—atheistic, plenty of love in the family, financial problems. Before I met her, somebody described her as the girl with the striped glasses, and I knew just who they were talking about, recalling her laughter I'd heard once in a bar, mirthful and genuine, a fat woman's laughter.

Her house was fat too, by which I mean it seemed to belong to a fat person. All the chair cushions always half on and half off, and the shawls thrown over the chair backs not quite hiding the tatty spots, and the runners askew on the wood floors. A hairbrush sat on the arm of a couch, and a bowl on the end table, Cheerios floating in milk, the spoon on the floor in the kitchen. The dolls wore real neckties. The children themselves were grass-stained and always pestering her and losing their shoes, but Carla just went along. She steered them toward the television, on constantly. That I never understood. My own house was clean, quiet, and orderly the way I still like it, and Carla's disorder astonished me. Once I saw her drop something and not pick it up. There was a room, an enclosed porch really, sliding off its foundation, that was filled with spider plants. She was picking the dead leaves out of the pots and weeding and then aerating the soil, loosening the roots with the tips of her fingers. A whole section of spider plant fell to the floor—soil, roots, weeds, leaves, and all. The weeds in particular fascinated me. My own potted plants sprouted delicate clovers and occasional stems of grass, while Carla's weeds were of a monstrous variety not even to be found outdoors. Their thick milky stems sported hirsute leaves of all colors, scarred with insect galls and opaque larval sacs. Even her soil was laced with a brilliant fungus. We both stared at the clump, and Carla prodded the fungus with a bare toe, but let it lie and went on chatting. Probably we were sharing our complaints about men; there weren't any good ones in town. Not that we minded personally, but we sympathized with anyone who did.

"They're all lumps," Carla said, and we went on describing a few and their various lumpish characteristics. The lumpiest of all was named Christopher Curtis—he was the one we joked about. Christopher affected a beatnik style but was too bald and desperate to carry it off. Actually he should have given up a long time ago but he was hanging on, and everyone watched in fascination as he courted local college women and took them to bed, after which they ran away from him. I worked in a restaurant he frequented and overheard a couple of his hip protestations. It was rumored that the college planned one day to demolish his house and build a parking lot. That was what Carla and I ended up talking about, the parking lot, and how ugly it would be on a residential street. Then one of the children screamed, and Carla yelled, "What is it?" with her arms still upraised among the spider plants. Oh, she was fat. She wore a long skirt with an uneven hem, and I could see that her ankles did not look like ankles at all. I never knew, at any given time, if she was pregnant or not. When she left the room, I picked up the watering can, and watering the ceiling plants indulged in the uncomplicated flexibility of my body. Then I gathered up the clump of spider plant, but at the sound of Carla's footsteps I put it back on the floor, because to pick up something at Carla's was like dropping it in mine.

Late one night Carla knocked on my window scaring the hell out of me with her thump-thumping. It was just like Carla to knock on a window instead of a door, but I didn't know that and I screamed so loud David ran down from the bedroom to rescue me. Later on I said, "Why didn't she just climb right in instead of knocking?" David said she wouldn't make it through the window. Poor Carla. It was my music box she wanted, a Greek thing my daughter liked to listen to, called a Kouvalias, with brightly painted wood balls affixed on springs around a central globe, so when the globe spun, the balls turned and undulated. Carla's youngest children, who loved the Kouvalias, had measles and weren't sleeping. She hoped it might comfort them. Could she borrow it?

I found it in its spot on the mantelpiece and handed it over. The Kouvalias played *Never on Sunday,* a strange song for a child's toy, to be sure, but cheerful and mischievous. The song is sung by whores; Sunday is their day off. Carla and I used to joke about this. Sunday was her day on, she said, she and her husband always had the greatest time on Sunday mornings. She used to sing along, as the notes sounded, with a voice as fat as the rest of her, and then go on to gloat about her husband. He was a public defender most eloquent in bed. *Equal Justice for All,* was how Carla described it. That night she wound the box up as she left, through the door, and sang for the benefit of the neighborhood. I laughed, and switched on the porch light, but I was distressed, as she walked off, to hear the music fade. Forever, I thought, knowing Carla. David and I took exacting care of our belongings, and when I'd lifted the Kouvalias from its spot there was not a ring of dust to show where it had stood.

Soon thereafter, my husband found work in another state and we made plans to move again. Our plans consisted of nothing more than a change-of-address at the post office, a week of meals designed to make use of all leftovers, and the assumption of a psychological limbo by which we gently disengaged ourselves from what had come to be home. Night by night, David washed and rinsed the day's dishes, pots, and pans, while I dried them, wrapped them in newspaper, and stacked them in a carton in a corner of our kitchen. We packed our clothing that way also, washload by washload, and our albums as well, saving for last those we played most often. This way, the house emptied; it seems to me now that this gentle, determined system of sorting and packing, reenacted so many times, has formed the rhythm by which David and I have lived.

I played the usual game with Carla. I simply told her we were leaving but then went on as if no such thing were happening. One evening that week, I dropped my daughter at a friend's house for dinner and stopped for a red light. Winter was coming, the traffic was slow, a near-freezing mist dropped out of the sky. David was home, putting dinner in the oven. As was usual during the final days of packing I was feeling impatient, so instead of waiting for the light to turn green I turned right and found myself on Carla's street. There I parked the car and made for her house, head bowed against the wet cold.

Carla's was a three-family house with a common entry. From the vestibule, where the families stored their tricycles, strollers, and boots, stairs led to the upper apartments, but Carla's door opened directly. Ordinarily it was left ajar, so that Carla had a view of who was coming and going, and so the upstairs tenants, on their way into and out of the building, might stick their heads in Carla's living room to see what was on TV. However, on this particular evening the door was closed. The vestibule's ancient radiator hissed and spat, and the damp, floppy linings of the unzipped boots steamed.

Removing my gloves, I knocked on the door and waited a minute. Nobody came. Then the radiator clanged and was still, and in the sudden quiet of the hallway I heard the children yelling, and Carla's own shouts clamoring above them for control.

"Well then, bring Lizzie your truck and then you can play with hers. *No, Theo.* I am *not* going to dry your hands, you're big enough to do it. This is crazy. She's not accepting it. Stop elbowing!"

Soon only one child screamed, the youngest. But the others never quite stopped jostling and whining, and I swear the door vibrated under my hand. I could feel Carla's patience waning.

So I opened the door and stepped in. It seemed the natural thing to do. At once I yelled, "Hello," and took off my coat and draped it round my shoulders. I nearly overlooked Carla's husband. He was slouched in an armchair. At first I supposed he was sleeping. But he was watching the television set, which wasn't on. He ran splayed fingers through his hair, drank beer, and sat there and did not acknowledge me, while in the adjacent room the skirmish renewed itself.

"I said stop elbowing," Carla pleaded, and the baby screeched with new force and astonishment. Something fell with a clang. Carla's husband drank away the head of his beer, then wiped the froth from his mouth with a sleeve and vomited. In a minute I was back in my car, sitting in the dark. "What gets me is this," I said later to David, over our dinner. "Did he come home and get the beer from the back porch and pour it into the glass himself, or did Carla pour it for him? Did she have it waiting for him when he got home? But there's no place to put a glass of beer in a house like that without knocking it over."

David chuckled. He had just told me that we weren't moving after all, not this week anyway, or the next, for he had been placed with another crew. Yet still I felt geared for the move and hoped vaguely not to see Carla again. When she phoned I went over there and said in an offhand way, "I came by the other night but the kids were screaming. Mike was watching television."

"Puking his ass off" was what Carla said.

In January Carla had a yard sale. The sale took place in the vestibule, since there was snow outside, but the sale goods spewed into the living room as well, making it difficult to discern exactly what was for sale and what wasn't. Carla seemed actually to decide these things on the spot, at the very last minute. When someone asked if she was selling the couch, she said, "Oh, no"; then, "Well, how much will you pay for it?"; then, "But I can't sell it. What would I tell Mike?"—because Mike was not supposed to know about the sale at all. He was squandering their money, in Carla's words. "He's squandering me, too," she said good-naturedly. The children had been ill through Christmas and kept Carla awake for nights needing rocking and stroking. Throughout, Mike dreamt with his head down under the sheets as if nothing could move him, and in the morning he told Carla his dreams. He said he'd dreamt she was thin, with a feather cut. Then he gave her twenty dollars for a dress to be bought when she'd lost some weight, and ten for the beautician.

"Ten!" Carla yelled.

She put the two bills inside a Whitman's chocolate box, fastened the box with a rubber band, and hid it, like a dog burying a bone.

It was the meagerness of this stash that encouraged Carla to plan the yard sale. Of course she had no intention of cutting her hair, which was coarse, long, and fuzzy with red highlights flashing fitfully, like sparks from a bunch of live wires. Nor did she seem to care about losing weight. The yard sale, she supposed, would provide her with several hundred dollars, and when she had this money, she would know what to do with it. Something long-term, she speculated. I feared she would bury it along with the rest, to be lost or thrown away by mistake. However, I was discouraged when only forty-two dollars' worth of stuff had been sold by noon on the day of the sale, and I stared around, hoping to find something to buy myself.

There was nothing, really. A heap of tenty clothing: smocks, caftans, voluminous duffel skirts and flimsy robes, all with failing seams, torn hems, loose buttons, and stained underarms, all Carla, Carla, Carla, as if she were still inside them, their pockets crammed with tissues and pistachio shells. Also stacks of mismatched dishes, lidless pots, and bent frying pans, all incongruously mixed, the boots with the pillows, the jars crammed with skeins of yarn, costume jewelry draped round the handlebars of a tricycle. I hit upon a thirty-cent sewing kit, containing several needles, some pins, no pincushion, no thimble, a few spools of pale tangled thread. For my daughter Jennifer, I thought. I'd give Carla a dollar and tell her to pay me back later—she never would.

Carla was laughing it up near the cash box, shaking the coins and chatting merrily with her customers, about childhood illness, crayon marks on plaster walls, burnt tea kettles, any number of small disasters. I had a premonition—there are people to whom bad things happen as a matter of course, and Carla was one of them.

Up I went with my traveling sewing kit, for I thought of everything in those days as a traveling this, a traveling that, and gave her the dollar, but Carla folded the dollar and handed it back, saying the kit was mine, she had meant to give me something anyway, for Christmas. Merry Christmas, she said, but I was not embarrassed for her. I looked at the kit and saw what I hadn't noticed, that the faint orange thread was not orange at all but a yellowed, aged white with a certain luster, really a lovely thing, like antique satin.

As I walked through the vestibule, I smiled; I imagined myself saying to David, "Come look at this threadbare thread," so I was smiling when I saw it, among a jumble of toys in a cardboard box. My Kouvalias. How abandoned it looked, the string from a pull toy tangled round the springs, but in good shape, really, still glossy and bright. The tag read three dollars. I brought it to Carla, just for a joke, to maintain my good spirits, and said I would take it.

"Oh, I can't tell you how much it kills me to have to sell this thing," Carla exclaimed. "I was hoping that no one would buy it! But come to think of it, three dollars—I don't think three dollars is enough for it, do you? It plays music, it's sort of an heirloom—I think five dollars, actually."

"Carla ..." I said, but she had wound the Kouvalias and held it high above her head so the others could hear, and sang along as usual; then, seeing my look of consternation, she said I could have it for four, a compromise. However I had only my dollar bill and a five. I gave her the five. Carla gave me the change in all sorts of nickels and dimes. Still I stood there, absolutely speechless—Carla could not bring herself to part with the toy. In fact she was so emphatic that I wondered if she knew. I had to wait until somebody purchased a lamp, distracting her, at which point she placed the music box on the table and I snatched it up and escaped. I was thinking, "You jerk, you *jerk,*" but I didn't know if that referred to myself or to Carla. At home I set it high on a shelf, not to be touched until several nights later, while Jennifer slept and David lay in bed, waiting for me. I prized that hour, when I alone was up, damp from the shower and dressed in a robe and slippers. Then I roamed from room to room and felt how glad I was. The rooms were brushed with quiet, neat and still. I did not turn on the lights, but the night sky glowed beyond the windows. There was the Kouvalias, so I wound it up and listened. A note was missing! It was the first syllable of "Monday" that was gone.

About this I complained on and off throughout the months: I should never have allowed her to take it, the children must have played handball with it, it was ruined, what a jerk I was, what a jerk Carla was.

Still, years later, if I wound the Kouvalias, I heard not the song but the missing note, like a gap in time and space, a brief, pinging silence.

I saw Carla only a few times more before early spring, when David and I moved away. She had made ninety-odd dollars with the yard sale, and with this money purchased a collection of unstrung beads from the estate of a deceased jeweler. Most of these beads were of glass, their insides awash with smoky whorls. All were quite old. A few were flat white and resembled melon seeds. Oddly, these delicate, modest ones were Carla's favorites; she had dug them out first, and strung them simply on strands of nylon thread, the clasp fashioned out of a loop of this thread and a seashell.

When Carla first showed me the beads, pulling open pouch after pouch behind the laundry area in the basement of her apartment building, she had not quite decided how to go about selling the finished product. In fact, she wore them herself, string upon string upon string, with a low-neckline blouse, so that the beads converged and fell between her breasts and disappeared. Carla laughed when she explained to me that Mike in his troubled state had failed to notice them. Mike had nearly lost his job, so he had cut down on his drinking, but still mooned about and slept defiantly in his armchair right after dinner. He seemed to have no interest in life, Carla said sympathetically. At night, if the children slept, Carla made her way down to the basement and stayed sometimes an hour, sometimes three, stringing beads with the aid of a naked bulb, her threads and pliers hidden in the shadow of the clothes dryer as it rumbled and spun. Now she pulled a length of thread from the spool, looped it round my neck to find the proper measure, cut it, knotted the end, and strung with intermittent bursts of concentration a Baggie-ful of multi-faceted globes, clear like prisms, of diminishing and then increasing circumference, so that the smallest were in the center and the largest at the clasp. This unusual necklace I imagined wearing against bare skin in summertime, wherever David and I might be, in a city, I imagined, perched on a fire escape to watch the sun go down, our paper plates balanced on our laps.

However, the beads were not for me—they were for Christopher Curtis, who lived in the would-be parking lot. He had noticed Carla wearing her beads, come up, and brazenly pulled them from their hiding place, so that they popped out of her cleavage one by one.

"That I couldn't believe!" Carla said. "I kept waiting for him to put them back. So anyway this is for him. He can give it to one of his pricky girl friends."

Then Carla put her finger to her lips, and the beads round her neck, for we were climbing the stairs again. Mike was not supposed to know about the hundreds of beads, because he hadn't known about the yard sale. How was Carla to suspect that a week later he would get it into his head to do a load of wash? Probably a guilt trip, Carla said. There he found the beads, the sacks and sacks, the finished strands wrapped up in scraps of velvet along with Carla's scribbled notes and the receipt from the jeweler's estate. How red in the face he was, when he finally came upstairs and threw beads like confetti round the house, out the back door like birdseed, and the rest in the garbage with an endless clatter. Oh, he was angry, and he wanted to know where she got the money. She said she'd borrowed it from me. So Mike came to our house and banged on the door, just as we were finishing our packing. We were to leave the next morning.

"Don't expect her to pay you back," he was yelling.

I assured him I wouldn't, for I knew what must have happened. Then I tried to shut the door, but in he came asking for beer. I sat him down with David in the kitchen, at the table piled high with our stuff.

David calmed him, I don't know how. They bitched about jobs, I think. I went next door, for our telephone had been disconnected, and called Carla to come and get him.

Carla said she couldn't, the children were asleep. Then she said, "Oh hell, I'll come, they'll survive," and showed up after nearly an hour.

"You gave him a beer," she said, and smiled slyly.

I smiled back.

That was good-bye.

Houston isn't really like the world at all, because it's hard to think of people actually living here and carrying on in normal ways when every time you turn around there's some cheap steak house with a giant plastic cow suspended above and in the distance or just around the corner a neon hamburger blinking like a UFO. The place isn't zoned, and the highways aren't wide enough to hold the traffic, and the trees are too small—they look like weeds. But there we were, David and I, making the best of things. David had a job that paid for some technical schooling, and I found myself manager of a shop that sold the kind of necklaces that Carla strung. Ironically, I thought of her every morning, faced with tiers of funky earrings and bracelets of dense, hammered brass.

The shop sold stationery also, in tutti-frutti colors, and boxes of notecards featuring elaborately attired penguins. For Jennifer I would take home a package of Raspberry paper, along with Lemon envelopes, contenting myself with the notion that my daughter would not be like me, with no one to write to, a history of casual friendships vacated like rental houses. In fact I began to suspect that it was not the friend that mattered but the habit of friendship, which followed me wherever I went, to be picked up where it had been left off but with some entirely new person. Already I'd discovered this person in Houston, a girl who worked in a bookstore down the road from my shop, who interested me precisely because we looked so much alike and were so alike in style. Unfortunately, I did not really like her. I found her too cool. Still, we met for lunch and sometimes walked each other home along the sunny, impersonal streets, trying to talk about things that mattered. Once, when we were to have lunch together, I was thrilled that she didn't show up, that she had forgotten—this might be an opportunity for the two of us to hate each other. I read through the menu, glanced at the door, read the menu again, glanced again at the door, did not order lunch, just a cup of coffee, fumed when it came, sipped it, stared hard at the door, but nothing happened, my fury would not mount. I was happy to be alone. In my bag was the Raspberry bond I'd intended for my daughter, so I opened the package, naturally, as if I'd known all along that I was going to write to Carla. I wrote: "Dear Carla, Here we are in Houston, trying to make the best of things. David's in school and I'm managing a sort of gift/jewelry shop. Jennifer is fine. This is her note paper. We've taken her twice to a place called Aransas, a wildlife refuge southwest of here, where the whooping cranes do their courtship dance. You can see them from the observation tower, jumping and flapping their giant wings, whooping I suppose, although you can't hear them."

And on about Aransas. The wild pigs, the tall grasses. I thought Carla would appreciate the whooping, and the snorting of the pigs. But she didn't write back, not for three months, and when she did it was with no reference to my news. She wrote, "Remember the beads?" and told me Mike had tripped on one, not long after we'd left town, and had injured his wrist.

Then she wrote "Phone on Friday night and ask Mike when my plane gets in. Tell him I'm staying an extra day, and that you're looking forward to seeing me."

And that was that. No explanation, no apology, not even money for the long distance call. And I would not do it, I would not, I would not, that is what I said to David, all night long. David was coughing that year, just a little, and I remember the sounds of that night. I won't do it—cough cough—I absolutely won't—cough—do it—cough cough.

I think now that if he hadn't been coughing, then I might not have done it, I might not have spent my resolve. Friday night came. I picked up the phone, I dialed, but Mike didn't answer, Carla did. She said, "No thank you, I already have a vacuum cleaner," and hung up the phone. Later on I laughed about the vacuum cleaner. Of course Carla did not have one, or if she did, she never used it.

David and I moved next to Minneapolis. David's health would not allow him to make the trip by car, so he flew on ahead with

Jennifer while I drove, pulling the U-Haul. We had accumu-
lated a few good pieces of furniture, more record albums, and
a decent stereo. Also the usual household goods, along with
some cherished items—photos of ourselves and of neat, sensi-
ble Jennifer, one or two sturdy house plants, some pottery and
other breakables, including the poor Kouvalias, wrapped up in
our winter sweaters. The trip took me close to where Carla
lived. I had not phoned, knowing that if Carla said she would
be there, she wouldn't be, and that if she said she wouldn't,
then she would and I would miss her. So there I sat, in my car
outside her house, when for the very first time it occurred to
me that she might not be at that house at all, she might have
moved away, to another city, even to Minneapolis itself. But out
I climbed, and in the vestibule I saw the same old boots, their
zippers still undone among piles of sandals. It was summertime, early evening, and the door to her living room stood ajar.

I looked in and saw her lounging on the couch with Christopher Curtis, kissing. I knew it was him because he hadn't
changed; he still looked too old, in his silly leather jacket and
scuffed blue jeans, but no older than the last time I'd seen him.
His hair had quit receding; he wore a chain round his wrist, his
fingers in Carla's hair. Her hair had been cut. It was a feather
cut, or in any case was meant to be, but the hair stood out in
coarse, shocked tufts in which the highlights winked and glit-
tered, like sparks in a forest after the fire, wanting to reignite.

"Carla," I said, and stepped inside, because I didn't care. I
meant to see her, talk, have dinner perhaps, and then drive
through the night. I decided this on the spot. I wanted to get to
David. We'd met a lady on the beach who told us it was pleurisy;
she heard his terrible coughing and came on over, her pockets
full of shells, and said to slather mustard on his chest.

However, it wasn't Carla, it was one of her daughters, who
looked up lazily and told me Carla wasn't home, she was out
on one of her tours. I did not know what this meant, exactly.
Chris was grinning behind his mustache, and the daughter

stood up and turned on the television. She was not as fat as Carla and moved in a sleepy, dreamy way. Behind her, the window was pocked with BB shots, a round of silent blasts. I wanted to laugh. I thought, if I wait, Carla won't come home, but if I leave, she'll be home in two minutes. I had thought I had come on a whim, but now I knew that I wanted something. Anything. Her street was lovely and familiar, with its tall, ungainly houses, its ratty lawns spilling out from cracks in the sidewalks, and not a single person in sight. So I stood in the vestibule, half-in and half-out, my face in the waning sunlight, and thought of something someone once told me. "I try not to go outside at dinner time," she said. "It makes me lonely."

That is how I remember my friends, if I remember them at all, in phrases and remarks that all seem to blend together as if I'd read them in a book. Someone once said, "I am not afraid of growing old; I intend to age gracefully," which is what I think of when I take my calcium tablets. Someone else said, "You shouldn't have to wait until your hair feels stiff to wash it, you can wash it when it's still clean," which is something I think of if my hair gets dirty. I remember the faces that said these things, but they are oddly disembodied and lifeless, as if they'd one day appeared, uttered a phrase, and dissolved. Carla was different; she had never said a thing worth saying again. I climbed into the U-Haul and followed her street to the end, then drove to the highway headed north. Later I stopped to eat, although I wasn't really hungry. I chose Howard Johnson's and sat at a high round stool at the counter, next to a candy display. My waitress, Dorothy, looked older than I was, but bouncy and keen, and didn't bother to write down my order. All I wanted was chowder and Coke, and saltines. Before the soup came I heard it, a penny someone dropped while paying at the register. It skidded on the carpet and struck the metal leg of my counter stool, with a fierce, loud *ping*.

I recognized it at once, the vagabond musical note, my long lost "Monday." It must have followed me to dinner, from Carla's.

Imagine Carla sugaring a cup of her tea, and the teaspoon striking the rim of her cup, and that note ringing out. Or one of the children (Carla's grandchildren) constructing one of those stringed instruments that children make, out of oatmeal cartons and rubber bands, and plucking the rubber band, and the first syllable of "Monday" twanging into the room.

Then Dorothy delivered my crackers, and I unwrapped the plastic and ate one whole before bending to pick up the penny. I dropped the coin on the counter and heard it again, *ping*.

And again, *ping*.

When the soup came I ate it at once, and got a hamburger as well, and ate that glancing all the while at the penny, which was smooth as it could be. I didn't touch it after a while. I left it lying on the counter along with the tip, for Dorothy.

Other Iowa Short Fiction Award Winners

1986
Eminent Domain, Dan O'Brien
Judge: Iowa Writers' Workshop

1986
Resurrectionists, Russell Working
Judge: Tobias Wolff

1985
Dancing in the Movies,
Robert Boswell
Judge: Tim O'Brien

1984
Old Wives' Tales,
Susan M. Dodd
Judge: Frederick Busch

1983
Heart Failure, Ivy Goodman
Judge: Alice Adams

1982
Shiny Objects, Dianne Benedict
Judge: Raymond Carver

1981
The Phototropic Woman,
Annabel Thomas
Judge: Doris Grumbach

1980
Impossible Appetites,
James Fetler
Judge: Francine du Plessix Gray

1979
Fly Away Home, Mary Hedin
Judge: John Gardner

1978
A Nest of Hooks, Lon Otto
Judge: Stanley Elkin

1977
The Women in the Mirror,
Pat Carr
Judge: Leonard Michaels

1976
The Black Velvet Girl,
C. E. Poverman
Judge: Donald Barthelme

1975
*Harry Belten and the
Mendelssohn Violin Concerto,*
Barry Targan
Judge: George P. Garrett

1974
*After the First Death There Is
No Other,* Natalie L. M. Petesch
Judge: William H. Gass

1973
The Itinerary of Beggars,
H. E. Francis
Judge: John Hawkes

1972
The Burning and Other Stories,
Jack Cady
Judge: Joyce Carol Oates

1971
*Old Morals, Small Continents,
Darker Times,*
Philip F. O'Connor
Judge: George P. Elliott

1970
The Beach Umbrella,
Cyrus Colter
Judges: Vance Bourjaily
and Kurt Vonnegut, Jr.